Hanging Johnny

Copyright © 1928 by D. Appleton and Company.

ISBN 979-8-218-54826-1

This edition published in 2025 by
Tough Poets Press
Arlington, Massachusetts 02476
U.S.A.

www.toughpoets.com

Myrtle Johnston
§
Hanging Johnny

Tough Poets Press
Arlington, Massachusetts

TO
MY MOTHER

They call me "Hanging Johnny"
(Away, boys, away!)
They say I hangs for money,
(Hang, boys, hang!)
                OLD SEA SHANTY.

Chapter I

The interior of the scaffold house grew suddenly brighter, as the sun broke through a bank of clouds, sending a triumphant shaft of light through a chink in the wall.

As if he sensed the sudden brightness, the condemned man lifted his head and a suggestion of hope came over his haggard figure.

"Will you take this white bag off of my eyes?" he said hoarsely.

For a moment no one answered.

The sheriff, the Governor and the others who were there to watch him die were looking towards the tiny spear of light, in a sudden silence. Only the executioner held his head down and fidgeted with the pinioning-straps round the man's legs.

Then the surgeon said gently: "It is better not."

"You brutes!" the man shouted. "Will you be denying me a last sight of the day?"

There was a desperate sob in his voice.

The chaplain stepped forward.

"No one denies you that, Tim Derrybawn," he said, and plucked off the white cap so that the man's face was exposed, brave, pale, excited, lifted eagerly to the sun. The executioner came forward very slowly and began to adjust the rope. His hand faltered a little as he slipped the ring behind the left ear. Then he put his hand on the bolt and the chaplain's voice rose thrillingly clear and impassioned in the last prayer for the dead.

"Wait!" cried the condemned man, "wait!"

The chaplain paused—he was saying the prayers, not reading them—and the executioner, with a look of something like hope, took his hand from the lever.

"What is the meaning of this?" said the sheriff.

"The reprieve! They'll be sending the reprieve, and God help us all if it comes too late." The prisoner's eyes were alight and he strained forward in the leather straps.

"This is the way he does be talking all the day," one of the warders whispered to the chaplain. "Always thinking of that reprieve he is. On the way from the cell he says to me: 'They can't delay with it any longer,' he says. But sure your reverence knows the way he does be talking. If it wasn't that I was in court and heard the evidence with my two ears, I'd be thinking myself it was not Tim Derrybawn who knifed Peter Connor in the club at Daly's."

A look of profound pity came into the chaplain's eyes. He bent towards the sheriff.

"We might wait," he said in a low voice.

"Not a scrap of use. The Home Office wouldn't consider his appeal for a moment. At his trial, his guilt was established beyond any doubt. The man Job Moran, especially, gave damning evidence. Poor devil, he's probably trying to gain time."

"Is it letting an innocent man die they are?" said the condemned man, and a slight fear showed in his voice.

Someone, one of the warders perhaps, gave a short laugh and the man's face blazed red.

"Found guilty, I was, in the court, and me as innocent as yourself, your honor. I swore in court, and I swear now, that I didn't kill

Peter Connor. But sure, I couldn't say the things I wanted, the way they did be asking me questions and arguing with each other. If they'd made me think I was guilty at the end of it all, there'd be no wonder in it at all."

"The hypnotism of a cross-examination," murmured the chaplain under his breath.

The sheriff opened his lips, but the man with the rope round his neck broke in again fiercely, vehemently.

"Peter Connor was a dirty dog of an informer, so he was, and I'd have liked mighty well to wring the lying throat of him. But I kept my hands off him, and it's the truth, as God sees me, that I don't know who it was knifed him that night over Daly's pub. I had the drink taken, God help me."

The sheriff stepped up to the executioner, who stood fingering an old, charred piece of rope he had taken from his pocket, his eyes still sullen and downcast.

"Better get it over quickly," said the sheriff in a whisper. "The man's raving. He's only trying to gain time."

The hangman moved slowly across to the lever again, putting back the old piece of rope. His head was still bent, and he walked in a curious, shambling way.

The prisoner turned to him, straining forward in his leather bonds. The colour had died off his face, leaving it white and panic-stricken.

"Johnny, you hypocrite!" he said huskily. "Begging me to confess in the cell, you were, the way you'd be sure you wouldn't be hanging an innocent man, and knowing all the while I was as innocent as my own child."

The hangman lifted his head as if he were going to speak. Then he looked away from the desperate eyes of the other man and said nothing.

"Me that was your friend," said Tim Derrybawn, "the only friend you had in the whole of this town. I wish I'd never taken up with you at all, so I do. Sure, didn't everyone in this town but myself know that there's no good in a man who does work the like of yours."

The warders and the surgeon's assistants were gaping at the singularity of the scene. It was like no other they had ever witnessed. The chaplain took a step forward and stretched out his arm to the prisoner, pointing his emaciated forefinger. It was a curious attitude, almost one of power and prophecy.

"Surrender yourself, Tim Derrybawn," he said. "Even now the Powers are preparing to avenge you and those who have suffered like you. And you perhaps are already the last in the world to die by the will of mankind."

There was a silence of amazement and bewilderment as the chaplain stepped back to his place. Even as they stared at him, wondering if they had really heard him speak, the light died out of his eyes, and his tall, gaunt figure seemed to shrink into itself again.

But, as the condemned man listened, a sort of fierce resignation came over his face.

"You're killing an innocent man," he said slowly, "and may God forgive you for it. Things the like of this shouldn't be let happen."

He turned his haggard eyes to the executioner.

"The curse of Heaven fall on you, Hanging Johnny, for the murder that's on your soul. For it's murder you're doing before God and the Saints. There's them outside will have your blood for this."

The hangman's hand faltered on the lever, and he let go his grasp on it.

"Slide that bolt and be damned to you," cried Tim Derrybawn.

"I'm not afraid to die. There's no sin on my soul, and God knows I am innocent."

The chaplain stepped forward, as if he were going to protest. Then he restrained himself and recited the last words of the prayer for the dead.

The hangman seized the bolt and swung it backwards with a heavy crash. The trap-doors under Tim Derrybawn's feet fell open.

Chapter II

"Mr. Cregan," said the sheriff.

The hangman moved across to him with that sullen, stooping walk of his.

"Mr. Cregan, I'm told there's a bit of a crowd outside the prison. They seem to be in rather a dangerous humour." He glanced at the drop and the taut rope, and abruptly looked away again. When next he spoke there was an inflection of something like contempt in his voice.

"Mr. Cregan, this execution seems to have roused a rather strong feeling against you. You had better not leave the prison yet, but if you will come with me, we will—arrange matters, now, and the Governor will see about a closed cab to your house. Extraordinary people these are in this country," he added under his breath, for he was an Englishman.

He left the house with the Governor and some of the warders. A few minutes later, the surgeon and his assistants followed him.

"Mr. Cregan," said the chaplain. "That was a terrible business."

The hangman turned fiercely.

"Will you leave talking of it for God's sake? I'm sick at my stomach because of the things I'm after seeing this day."

The priest studied him gravely for a few minutes.

"What made you choose the office of executioner?" he asked

presently. "You don't look fitted for the work."

The hangman had a pale, ascetic face with delicate, very clear-cut features. His nose was long and sensitive and slightly pinched at the nostrils. It seemed to quiver like a dog's when he smelt anything in the air. The chin was fine and pointed and he had a beautiful, emotional mouth. The whole face was poetic and classical in outline, though the hair that was brushed off his low, broad forehead was black and utterly unkempt.

"I was reared for the work," he said, "and my father an executioner before me. His name it was got me the post, I sometimes think. He's dead now, God rest him."

"But you dislike the office?" persisted the chaplain, as if he found Johnny Cregan an interesting study.

"Maybe I do, now, and yet—" He let his eyes wander to the drop where all that was mortal of Tim Derrybawn hung at the end of a rope, and the priest understood in a moment all the awe and fear and the irresistible fascination the work held for this man.

As they stood in silence, a faint noise came to them like the beating of drums. It grew nearer and they could distinguish shouts, angry and menacing, as if a great crowd were hammering at the prison walls.

"God!" said the hangman, and he moved nearer to the priest. "It's tearing me to pieces they'd be if they got me out there." A green tinge began to creep under his pale skin, and he shuddered. "You wouldn't get them to believe Tim Derrybawn was guilty, not if you brought the Archangel Gabriel with the Book of Sins, and it written there that 'twas he knifed Peter Connor, as black as print, so you wouldn't."

The priest looked quickly at him, but there was no humour in his face, only a tortured fear.

"And they want to avenge his death on you?" said the chaplain. Something in his eyes made the hangman shrink away from him.

"That's not it," he cried. "Oh God, they're out for my blood, because I'm after hanging a man that was my friend." His voice grew hoarse—"the only friend I had in the whole of this town."

The priest put his hand on the man's shoulder with a certain sympathy and understanding.

"Why did you do it?" he asked steadily.

"Because I was down and out. I owed money to every shop in the town. Sure, I hadn't a penny to buy the Police news the way I could see if there were any executions for me. Then I heard they were going to hang Tim Derrybawn, and—God forgive me—I applied for the job. I thought then—heavens above, I thought he was guilty, and 'twould be no sin on my soul. The whole of last night I was awake, praying to be able to do it. It's the first time I ever hanged a man of this town."

"And then—" said the chaplain very softly, as if he were afraid of breaking the man's current of thought.

"Then I'd have given the eyes of me to see him reprieved. I wouldn't have cared a damn if I'd only got the half of my money, or never set eyes on it at all, so I wouldn't. I made Tim think I thought 'twas guilty he was, for I wouldn't like him to know I was hanging him and knowing he was innocent. When he spoke up and swore 'twas not him that had killed Peter Connor, I knew he was speaking the truth. But, sure, your reverence knows it too. You know Tim Derrybawn was innocent."

The chaplain bowed his head.

"I knew it, and the world shall suffer for it."

"What do you mean?" whispered Johnny.

The noise of the vast crowd became deafening. Two words were shouted over and over again.

"What name do they call you?" said the chaplain.

A draught of air blew into the scaffold house, and the rope stirred, ever so gently. "What did Tim Derrybawn call you?"

A sullen look came over the hangman's face—the look of one who is shamed by his fellow creatures, and us ashamed of it.

"'Hanging Johnny' is the name they put on me in this town; sure, doesn't every man and woman in it know the work I do? The childer do be shouting it after me in the streets."

"Hanging Johnny," repeated the chaplain thoughtfully.

"From a song they took it. The sailors do be signing it on the ships below in the harbour."

"Have you the song, Johnny Cregan?"

The man turned away, the unhappy ashamed look still on his face and in his blue, bleak eyes.

"Och, I wouldn't like to be singing it to your reverence at all. It's a wicked, heathen song. A sailor's song."

He stole another glance at the gaping drop.

"Tim, if so be he's in Purgatory, will be putting a curse on me." His face was suddenly childlike in the throes of a child's fear. It was a strange destiny that had made this ignorant, sensitive creature an executioner.

The chaplain said:

"How do you know this is the first innocent person who has died at your hands?"

"Don't be talking like that. Sure, haven't I the right to live, the same as yourself, Father? Would you be taking away my living from me?"

"There are other trades!"

"I'm a cobbler," said the hangman, passionately. "I have a cobbler's shop down by the quays. But it's scarcely a *thraneen* that I make out of it. The people of this town don't like to be coming to my shop."

"And you will have to go away now. Your life won't be worth living after what has happened to-day."

"I'll go away," said Johnny slowly. "Maybe, I'll give up this work. I never thought anything about it before, but it seems now as if I could never handle a rope, but Tim's face would come before me, and the throat of him swollen. Oh, I wish to God I was in England! They say the executioners there have a fine easy time of it, by reason of the English people not interfering with the Courts of Justice and them that carry out the law."

"One day," said the chaplain, "there will be no Courts of Justice and no murder authorised by the law."

Johnny stared, and the chaplain began to sway on his feet.

"I hear the voice of God in my sleep. Very faint it is, like water far away, but sometimes the words come to me: 'Vengeance is Mine, I will Repay!'"

The priest's face was white, and his eyes were like two black holes bored into it. They glimmered with a queer light like a flame. His whole face had changed, and become rapt and visionary.

"'I will punish the wrongdoers,' says the Lord. It is not fit that man should take retribution out of the hands of God, and He is angry."

"What are you saying?" whispered Johnny, cowering back from this thing he could not understand.

"We should leave the punishment of murderers to the heavens above. We have only the puny one of death for all classes of evil-doer. But He would punish each according to the depths of his sin. I am the prophet of God, and He has sent me to convert the world."

"Sure, they wouldn't be afraid of them sorts of punishment at all," said Johnny, feeling he was on familiar ground, and less afraid.

"You fool! The punishments of God are worse than anything we could conceive. That rope! What is it, compared to the sufferings He could send upon us!"

He flung his arms above his head, the prophetic fury carved into his face like marble.

Horrified, Johnny shrank farther away from him. There was a slight noise outside, and a warder rushed in.

"Mr. Cregan, they're after dispersing the crowd. There's a closed cab waiting beyond for you." His face was pale and there was a look of fear in his eyes.

The priest strode forward.

"Why do you look like that? What has happened?"

"A terrible thing, your reverence." The man started back, frightened at the glare in the eyes close to his.

"The man Job Moran has confessed to the police. They're after arresting him. 'Twas he killed Peter Connor, after giving evidence at Tim Derrybawn's trial and all. He was wild to be in time to save Tim, so he was. When they told him he was too late, he fainted. It's a terrible bad job, your reverence, the whole of this thing."

"My God!" said Johnny Cregan. The warder stared at him. He had never seen Hanging Johnny at work before, and in the midst of his horror and amazement and excitement it flashed across him that here was a very odd executioner.

"'Twas Tim Derrybawn disremembering what he did that night, by reason of him being drunk at Daly's, that made it so easy for Job," he continued wildly. "And Tim couldn't deny the words he said, and many people listening to him. 'I'd like to get my hands on that dirty devil of an informer,' he said, meaning nothing at all,

God help him."

"But Job was safe," muttered Johnny. "Why in the name of the Saints did he confess to the police?"

"It's a mighty queer thing, Mr. Cregan. He said he couldn't sleep at night."

The priest had been standing erect, his wild eyes fixed on space, as if he indeed saw spirits and the fiery angels of his dreams.

When the warder said this, however, he turned quite calmly to Johnny.

"Job Moran preferred to be hanged rather than not be able to sleep," he said. A flicker of triumph shone for a second in his eyes. Then it was replaced by something which had not been there for the past ten minutes.

It was sanity.

Chapter III

The white road stretched away and away until it seemed to merge into the sky.

Celandine and speedwell bloomed on either side, lifting their heads to the sun.

Vast tracts of gorse lay on the right, looking like sheets of gold in the hard glare of heat. To the left the vague outlines of mountain peaks shimmered against the sky.

Johnny Cregan walked ankle-deep in fine, white dust. It blew all over him, so that his shabby coat looked grey, instead of black.

He walked steadily, keeping his eyes on the ground, where his shadow moved before him, a queer, hunched-up silhouette against the white road. Occasionally he wiped his face with a large green handkerchief, for he was not used to exercise, and the bundle he carried on his back was heavy. There was not a house in sight, and he saw no one except two men and a woman in an outside car that clattered past him once, the driver humming snatches of song under his breath.

They took no notice of the tall, lonely figure in its ragged clothes, and he wondered if they knew he was Hanging Johnny who was never going to hang anyone again.

The sun dropped lower and a fresh breeze lifted the hair on his temples. He stared anxiously along the road, but not a roof broke the monotony of the rolling, gorse-covered miles.

He was very tired, so he dragged himself to the bank on one side of the road, and opened his bundle. There was bread and meat inside, and a little silver. The sun was sinking, flinging a lovely riot of colour across the sky. The silvery peaks in the distance were splashed with bloodred light. Tongues of palpitating fire trailed themselves across the heavens till they merged into pink and turquoise.

Johnny leant his chin on his hands and watched, with all the starved, worshipping soul of him in his eyes.

Far, far behind him, Tim Derrybawn was dead, buried in the prison yard. But that memory could not dim the ecstasy he felt at being alone with the fire in the sky, and the gorse and the creeping twilight.

Johnny woke in the morning after a heavy, dreamless sleep. There was a pink light in the sky and he sat up to watch it.

From habit, little thrills of terror and excitement ran up his spine, for to him sunrise had been always a rather terrible thing.

He did not know what he was going to do. Perhaps he would find a village where he would earn money to pay his way up to Dublin. In Dublin he would get work, and he would make friends. He had never had any friends. But he was not thinking of this now. He was not thinking of anything, as he sat brooding and motionless, with his hands hanging between his knees, watching the sun climb over the edge of the world.

Presently he looked round for his bag, and found it open. With vague misgivings he put his hand in and searched among miscellaneous things. The bread and meat and the little heap of silver were gone.

For a second he stared in dismay. The bracken round him was

trodden down, and there was a hint of footsteps.

Then he shrugged his shoulders, and a smile softened his mouth.

"Bad cess to them tinkers! But sure it's no more than I asked for, sleeping the way a volcano wouldn't wake me. Maybe they were hungry too."

He put his hand in his pocket and drew out the old charred piece of rope. It was made of Italian silk hemp, and there was a ring at one end.

"The Lord be praised, they left this on me," he muttered; and clenched it tightly in his hand. A robin flew down from the top of a gorse bush and hopped close to him, its eyes shrewdly cocked.

"You wee impudent rapscallion, you!" Johnny coaxed, delighted at its confidence. "You have a hungry look on you." He searched again in his baggage and a few crumbs of bread came to light. He held them longingly for a second. Then he threw them all to the bird, watching, with a tender, half-pitiful smile while it devoured them. Presently he rose to his feet.

"Well, I'll be, saying good-bye to you now, my little rogue, though it's a fine, comfortable place I have of it here. I wouldn't say but I'll get some work in the next town, if so be there's any work for the likes of me in the whole of this country."

Feeling rather cramped and stiff, he stepped on to the road, swinging his burden to his shoulder. The sun was climbing higher and the heat was scorching. Johnny tramped steadily along, the sound of his feet breaking the silence like the beat of a hammer. Great boulders lay on either side of him, half smothered in heather. Now he began to sense a subtle change in the atmosphere. The place was utterly lonely. An indefinable air of sadness hung over the wilds of gorse and bracken, as if something terrible had happened there long ago. Even the blazing sunlight could not take the desolation from the rocks that rose like the masts of derelict ships from a yellow sea.

Hour after hour he trudged on, eating up the miles under his dusty, torn boots.

A group of clouds hung low in the north. Sometimes they looked like the outlines of mountains, and sometimes like gigantic figures. On and on through the awful heat and the solitude. Johnny did not know where he was. He could only go forward, almost praying every time he turned a corner that he would see a house, or a living creature on the other side.

The silence in this place was like death. He lifted his head suddenly as a sound came to him. It was like the footsteps of two people running hard, and Johnny almost covered his eyes with his hands.

Round a bend in the road came a donkey, trotting valiantly under the weight of a stout woman and two baskets.

He was so relieved that he gave a shout. He stood in the middle of the road, and, rather angrily, she eased up beside him.

"Begging your pardon, ma'am, could you tell me the way to the nearest town?"

She stared at him with suspicion and a trace of fear.

"Praise be to God, I've met someone at last!" he added. "The loneliness here is terrible."

"Few people do be going up and down on this road," said the woman. "'The Place of Spirits' is the name they put on it beyond there."

She bent forward and looked carefully at him. "Man, who are you? I wouldn't say but I've seen your face before this."

"My name's Cregan, ma'am," said Johnny without reflecting. "Johnny Cregan."

Her face blanched with fear.

"Glory be to God, it's the Hangman! It's Hanging Johnny! Musha, musha, this to happen to me"—she gave the donkey a resounding slap and it bounded forward—"me that has never broken a fast!"

"What's come to you at all?" Johnny tried to catch the bridle, and she gave a scream of fear.

"Let go of me, you murdering blackguard! The Lord save us and help us, he's going to knock me down!"

"Will you listen, ma'am? I'm after resigning—"

"In this place of all places. Let go of me, you bloodthirsty ruffian, or I'll knock the five senses out of you."

She slapped the donkey again and it plunged forward, tearing the bridle out of Johnny's hands.

He watched her dazedly and rather bitterly as she galloped away from him, still praying for protection, until she dwindled to a black speck against the horizon.

The Place of Spirits! Shuddering a little, Johnny glanced round him. Some distance away he saw huge, gaunt stones rising up sharply from the heather. Some of them were broken, and three had fallen and lay like dead giants, but he could see that they had once formed a circle.

Even in the indifferent daylight there was something sinister about them. They were full of a subtle menace.

Johnny put his hands in his pockets and tramped on, keeping his head bent to shut out the sight of them.

A gnawing hunger began to torment him, and his head swam in the heat.

When next he looked up, hills were rising on either side of him—brown, rugged hills with boulders flung carelessly on them, and trees that looked like patches of hair.

The sun dropped behind him, and the mountain peaks began to shine like silver. From the trees came the discordant, sorrowful cry of a jay.

Johnny's feet felt as if they had lead weights tied to them. A nail had pushed itself up through the sole of his boot, and was hurting him so unbearably that he had to take the boot off and throw it into the ditch.

His throat was coated with dust and he peered anxiously into the ditch at one side of the road to see if a drop of water remained. But it had all been dried up.

He raised his heavy eyes and saw that the road in front of him sloped up a steep hill. For a moment he wanted to fling himself down on the grass and sleep until he died. Then he set his lips rather sternly and began to climb the hill.

The sun beat down on his head, making the blood in it throb.

He drew laboured, painful breaths as the stones tore his bare foot and made it bleed. He did not know that he was challenging his destiny.

When he reached the top he could scarcely stand, but he put down his bag and looked eagerly for what lay on the other side.

Then he gave a hoarse, exultant shout. Below him, an untidy village sprawled over half a mile. There was a main street with shops on either side, and beyond that were little brown houses with thatched roofs, and a grey chapel.

He could see people, loitering in lazy, friendly groups, on the street.

A feeling of exhilaration came over him, and he strode down the hill as steadily as he had walked in the morning.

Presently he reached the bottom and began to walk along the

street. Some of the shops were real ones with plate glass windows and a counter, and others were cottages with some bottles of sweets displayed in one of the windows.

As he walked along the exhilaration faded away, and his foot began to cause him agony. Some of the people glanced curiously at him. Their eyes were friendly, but Johnny's sensitive mind found distrust and mockery in them. He shrank into the shadows of the houses, trying to escape them.

He did not dare to go up to any of the little two-storied houses and ask for work.

He was morbidly self-conscious, and he felt with shame that he had no right to be in this town where he did not belong.

His feet were so heavy that he could scarcely drag them along the rough, hot road.

At last he came to the end of the street. The corner house on his side was a grocer's shop. It was larger than any of the others and it had a look of prosperous respectability that made it different from the rest.

Scarcely knowing where he was going, Johnny turned the corner, and came face to face with a woman.

She was leaning on a low, iron gate, with her arms folded on the topmost rail.

She wore a brown sunbonnet and was humming a lively little song to herself.

She regarded the world that lay beyond her garden gate with a contented expression. Behind her lay a small flower garden with beds of geraniums and lobelias, and very neatly kept grass.

Almost unconsciously Johnny stopped to look at her. Something clean and honest about her attracted him after the frightening walk through the Place of Spirits.

Suddenly she turned her head and saw him. A faint red crept up her neck and cheeks, and he saw she was going to be rather angry because he was staring at her.

"Have you—have you any work that wants doing, ma'am?" he asked wistfully.

She had turned away again, and did not see the nervous, speechless appeal in his eyes.

"We don't like our work done by beggars," she said crisply.

The words left him breathless as if they had been a douche of cold water.

He felt the colour stinging his face as he turned and went blindly down the road.

Then, his foot slipped, he fell heavily, and could not get up. In a moment he heard running footsteps, and an arm was round his shoulders, raising him from the ground, a firm, plump arm, with a strong hand that forced him back when he tried to rise.

It was the woman.

"Are you hurt?" she said. "Move your ankle."

He moved it, and the pain was excruciating.

"I thought so," she said calmly; "you've twisted it."

Johnny opened his eyes and gazed into the capable, comely face.

"Where do you live?" she asked him in a business-like way.

"I—I don't know," he said helplessly.

"Then I'd better take you to the house. Try to get up. Steady, steady, not so fast. I've got you."

Johnny struggled in agony to his feet.

"My bag?" he whispered. "Have you got my bag?"

"I have it here. Walk slowly now."

The arm that supported him never faltered or gave way. He

leaned his weight on it and felt the muscles tighten under the firm flesh. As they reached the gate, he spoke faintly.

"Are you bringing me into the garden?"

"Yes," she said.

She lifted the latch, and a moment later he heard the gate shut with a clang behind him.

Chapter IV

In the evening Anna Murphy stood in a room over the grocer's shop.

She had let down her hair and was combing it in front of her mirror.

She parted it carefully and threw it back over her shoulders. Then, as she caught sight of her face in the glass, she paused, and perhaps for the first time in her life stared long and rather wistfully at her reflection.

She was tall, and she had a splendid, unrestrained figure. Her face was rosy and red-lipped, full of practical good sense. The eyes were black under a high, capable forehead.

Anna stared and laughed.

"Why, I'm pretty, and I never realised it before."

She was so amazed at the miracle of her animal health and good looks that she actually dropped the comb. Then with another laugh at the vanity which was so unlike herself, she flung the mass of dark, rippling hair over her face again and began to brush it with great energy and efficiency.

When this was done, she parted it again in the middle, and drew it tightly off her forehead, not caring that the waves were all being flattened out and destroyed.

A few little stray curls she ruthlessly pinned out of sight, without bestowing another glance in the mirror.

Then she went downstairs, looking very clean and neat and smooth.

In the parlour off the shop her father was sitting, smoking his pipe by the empty fireplace. Anna stood in the doorway.

"Well, father," she said, "I'm ready."

James Murphy glanced up and smiled at her.

"You're looking nice, Anna."

She closed the door carefully and came across to him.

"Where are the accounts, father? I want to go over them with you."

He took some rather shabby books from the desk, and Anna pulled up a chair and found a pencil. Her father began to go through the books, but presently he lay back and watched, with a half-satisfied, half-amused smile, as she settled herself to the work, glad to have it all to herself.

For half an hour there was silence, as her capable pencil totted up column after column, writing sometimes in a neat, clear hand.

At last, she put the pencil back in the tray and closed the books.

"I've finished. Would you like to look through them, father?"

She brought one or two for his inspection, and he glanced over them, still with that satisfied little smile.

"You're a good bookkeeper, Anna. Your schooling taught you figures, if it taught you nothing else."

"Yes," she said composedly, "arithmetic was the only lesson I liked. The others seemed so useless."

"So I took you away from school, and you but a wee girleen, to learn you to keep house," he chuckled. "You were never one for books, Anna."

"No, I don't like reading. It's such waste of time."

She went to a table, took from it a large work-basket and began to thread a darning needle.

"Must you be working all the evening?" he asked rather wistfully.

"There are all these stockings of yours, father. They must be done to-day, and I hadn't time yesterday."

"Bless the child, I don't care a pig's tail about the stockings."

She did not trouble to answer this absurd remark, and presently he added with a certain longing:

"Anna, won't you come here and talk to me? I feel I'd like to speak to you about the shop."

She moved her chair a little nearer to him.

"I can talk while I'm darning, father."

For a moment he watched her busy fingers guiding the needle through the strands of wool. Then he said abruptly:

"How old are you, Anna?"

"Twenty-four, father. Don't you remember my twenty-fifth birthday is next month?"

"Ah, so it is. A fine woman you're growing, Anna. I'm proud of you."

"I'm so glad, father." She darned industriously, her dark, shining head bent over the needle.

"After your twenty-fifth birthday, you'll be taking the shop into your own hands," said James Murphy.

"That will be grand, won't it, father! I'm just longing to begin. I've always wanted to see if I could run the shop entirely on my own."

"Well, you're young, Anna. But, sure, I wouldn't wonder if you know as much about business as your old father." He leant back, watching her as she snipped off a piece of wool and threaded her needle again. "I'm growing old," he said presently, "and I'll be glad to hand the whole thing over to you. It will be grand to watch you handling it, Anna, and wondering what you'll make of it. It's what I've always planned for you."

"And—things have been a little slack lately, haven't they, father? I'll liven it up, and there's a lot of changes I want to make. I'll get rid of Breenan. He isn't much use, and I'm sure I could manage quite by myself. I wish we could afford to buy out Johnson. We'd have nearly all the trade in the town, then."

Her face had flushed with enthusiasm, and her eyes were shining. Presently she rose to her feet, energetic, youthful, splendidly self-confident.

"That reminds me, father," she said, "a man—a poor, wretched tramp—fell outside our gate this afternoon and sprained his ankle, so I brought him in. He doesn't seem to live anywhere, poor creature."

"He can stay here till he's all right," conceded James Murphy.

"Of course he ought not to be tramping the roads. A man like him should be able to get work. I hate to see strong, able men begging; it's so disgraceful. But perhaps when he's better, I can give him some work in the garden."

"I leave that to you, my dear," said James Murphy. He got up and, taking both her hands, pulled her down on the arm of his chair.

"Anna, tell me. Are you ever going to get married?"

"Of course I am, father. I want a home of my own and children. Sons."

"You've had plenty of chances," he observed.

"Yes, I suppose so, but I've never thought about it much. I don't want to marry yet. I'll have my hands full with the shop."

"What sort of man would you like for your husband, Anna?"

"Oh, I haven't thought. A decent, hardworking man who wouldn't want to kiss me."

He laughed, and she coloured a little because she did not know why.

"You'll never find a husband like that, Anna."

"Oh, well," she stood up and disengaged her hands. "We needn't bother about it yet, need we? Good gracious!" with a glance at the clock, "it's half-past nine!"

"Yes; it's getting dark. You'd better bring in the candles."

"Why, it's bed-time, father, and we mustn't stay up later. We don't want to waste candles."

She did not kiss him, and he did not seem to expect it.

"Good night, father."

"Good night, Anna."

She picked up her work-basket and went quietly out of the room.

Chapter V

One morning, a week later, Johnny felt himself able to get up and dress.

The pain and the nervous exhaustion had passed away. The sunlight streamed hopefully through the window into the narrow, little bare room where he lay. It had whitewashed walls, a narrow, iron bedstead, and a tin basin filled with cold water. Johnny sat up and rolled back the blankets. His own coat, neatly mended, lay on a chair, but the trousers and shirt were not his, and the brown boots and dark green socks were strangers to him.

He looked at them dubiously. Then he got up and began to put them on.

When he was dressed, he looked round for his bag and saw it on the floor, unopened, just as he had seen the woman put it down.

Then he opened the door and ventured into the passage. There was a flight of stairs leading down, wooden and bare at the top, covered with a dark red carpet farther down.

As he stood hesitating someone came up the stairs and stood facing him.

"Good morning, Miss Anna," he said shyly.

"I'm glad to see you up. How do you feel?"

She was looking very fresh and robust in a mauve, checked gingham dress, with her brown sunbonnet.

Johnny gazed admiringly at her, and she grew a little pink.

"Do you know," she said, "I don't know your name. You were so ill, I forgot to ask you."

This time he reflected.

"Johnny Croghan," he said.

"Well, Johnny," she said quite casually, using his Christian name as she would to a servant: "What are you going to do now?"

"I'm blest if I know," he confessed stupidly.

"Did you live near here?"

"A fair distance away," he evaded.

"What sort of work are you looking for?" persisted Anna, bent on gaining some impression of his character.

"Sure, I don't care much. Maybe I could do outdoor jobs," he looked at her pleadingly, and she gave him a straight, rather puzzled glance.

"You don't look very strong."

"Och, there's nothing the matter with me," he contradicted eagerly.

She was too ignorant to find any meaning in the way his hand quivered and clenched itself on the banisters. It was a long, sensitive hand, with tapering, pale fingers.

"Well, do you want to stay here, Johnny, or would you rather go somewhere else for work? We can only afford to have our jobs done very well, or not at all."

She spoke severely, but she smiled at the same time, showing strong, white teeth.

"I'd like to be staying here, Miss Anna, if so be you have any work I could do. May God bless you for being so kind to me, and me no better than a man off the streets."

She laughed a little at that, and he continued, shyly, because of her laughter: "Miss Anna, was it you gave me these good clothes? Ought I to be wearing them at all?"

"They belonged to father, Mr. Murphy. I couldn't let you wear those rags again, because you'll have to look respectable if you're working in our garden. Everyone can see it from the road. I had to mend your coat because Mr. Murphy couldn't spare you one."

"Is it me work in the garden?" he marvelled.

"Well, it's this way. We always do the garden ourselves. I do at least, when Mr. Murphy's at the shop. So, you see, we can't afford to pay you for doing it, when we can manage ourselves for nothing. But if you like to take the work off our hands, we'll give you your food and a bed. Would you care to do that?"

Johnny made an effort, and stopped watching her face.

"Sure, I would, Miss Anna, thanking you kindly. But it's little though I know about plants and flowers and them things."

"I'll show you," she said briskly. "Come along."

She walked down the stairs ahead of him, glad, though she could not have told why, that he had not refused her not very tempting offer.

He followed her through the side door and into the conventional, flowery little plot of ground, attached to the grocery store.

"These geranium beds need weeding," she explained. "Pull out all the blades of grass and the groundsel. This is groundsel," she pointed out furtive green sprays among the fiery-petalled flowers and he duly examined and identified them.

"Then you must pull all the dandelion roots and daisies out of the grass. Don't throw away the dandelion leaves. We can use them for salad. Do you understand what you have to do?"

"Yes, Miss Anna."

"You'll find a fork in that shed, if you want one."

She turned and walked back to the house, humming a little song. Johnny stared after her, admiring her swinging, purposeful walk.

As she reached the door she glanced over her shoulder at him, but when she saw his eyes fixed on her, she abruptly looked away again, and wished she had not let him see.

James Murphy was in the back parlour when she came in.

"Father," she said, "I told Johnny—his name is Johnny Croghan—he can work in the garden and we'll give him his food and let him sleep here. I wouldn't pay him anything, of course."

"Why, Anna, you always do the garden yourself. I don't call it work. Strikes me the fellow is going to be a visitor, and have a fine, easy time of it. That's not like you, Anna."

To his surprise she turned on him, her cheeks crimson.

"It's my business, father. You said you'd leave it to me. I wish you wouldn't interfere."

"Come, Anna girl, what's the matter with you?"

He tried to stroke her hair, but she jerked her head away and went through the connecting door into the shop.

Chapter VI

In the days that followed, Johnny was happier than he had ever been in his life.

His work was very light and he loved the long hours out of doors in the sunshine. The morbid, dark years lay behind him like a shadow. He had left them in the Place of Spirits. But they had eaten into his soul, and he dreamed of them sometimes at night.

Often Anna would come out and sew on the little bench outside the door. Then she would talk to him, and he would answer crudely and awkwardly, but with a great, eager gladness inside him.

At first he did not dare to stop working when he talked to her, for she always said, "Johnny, get on with that digging. I shall have to go in if you stop working directly I come out."

But as the days wore on, he could lean on his spade with idle hands while she asked him questions, and she never remonstrated. Perhaps she did not see him, for she always bent her head rather low over her work. One half holiday, James Murphy strolled out to have a look at the flowers.

Johnny did not hear him approach and was sitting on the grass, brooding and silent, twisting a geranium in his hands.

"What are you doing?" said James Murphy. Johnny got to his feet and regarded the angry, red face.

"How dare you sit like that doing nothing! How dare you pick our flowers!"

He was so angry that Johnny was a little puzzled. He picked up his spade again, and James Murphy turned and went into the house.

Here he met Anna with a bundle of white sewing in her arms.

"Where are you going?" he said.

"Into the garden, father."

"Keep an eye on that fellow out there. He'll be lying on the grass, smoking his pipe as soon as your back's turned. And he'll do worse than that."

"What do you mean, father?"

"He looks a low scoundrel. I wouldn't trust him farther than I'd swing an ox by the tail. Stealing our flowers—"

"What nonsense," she broke in impatiently. "You know perfectly well Johnny wouldn't dream of doing anything like that."

"Well, anyway, he's about finished everything there is to be done in the garden. He is simply wasting his time now."

"Then he can help you in the shop."

Murphy almost exploded with wrath.

"I wouldn't have him in the shop for ten minutes. I never trust a man with eyes his colour."

"I don't see why you're so down on him, father. I can find something else for him to do."

"There's something about him maddens me. He will go out of the house to-morrow."

"He shall not!"

Both were thoroughly angry. Anna faced him for a moment, her head thrown back defiantly. Then she marched past him, and out into the garden.

And Johnny stayed on, still doing odd jobs. Anna gave him two chairs to mend, and he worked at them laboriously and not very skilfully.

One day when she came out he held a bunch of geraniums, tied up with raffia.

"Miss Anna, I was thinking you might like these for your room. I'm after picking them from the back where they won't show."

The colour shot into her face.

"Johnny, you know we never pick our flowers. It spoils the beds and they're an extra trouble in the house."

He looked very miserable, and she added suddenly, "Give them to me, Johnny. I do like them. Thank you so much. They will look pretty in my room."

He muttered something unintelligible, but his eyes were radiant.

Anna sat down on the bench, laying the flowers on her knee.

"Johnny, you're beginning to look shabby again. Haven't you one other coat of your own? What have you in that sack of yours if not clothes?"

She saw a shadow come over his face and his eyes looked fearful.

"I haven't a clo belonging to me, Miss Anna. There's only—rubbish in that bag."

She was not a tactful woman.

"Why do you carry rubbish about with you—"

"Look at the butterfly, Miss Anna. It's after sitting on your head as proud as the king himself. There, it's gone away."

A big Red Admiral flew past her face, and she did not refer to the bag again. But she found herself thinking of it, while she fried the sausages for supper. It weighed so heavily on her mind that, going upstairs, she passed Johnny's room mechanically. The door was open and the bag had been dragged into the middle of the floor and left untied. Curiosity overcame her and she tiptoed into the room. The mouth of the bag gaped open and she bent down to look in.

She saw a broad leather belt, four narrower straps, and a long coiled-up rope.

She did not know what they were, but the sight of them gave her a vague horror. She knew with strange instinct that she must never speak about them to Johnny.

Chapter VII

Johnny was watering a bed of lobelias. He held a large jar, the contents of which he flung over the flowers in a heavy sheet of water, very unlike rain. When it was empty, he filled it again from a tap in the wall by the side door.

He worked fitfully and lazily in the brilliant sunshine. No rain had fallen for the past week.

As he was filling the jar at the tap, he heard Anna and her father in the passage. The door was open and their voices floated out to him distinctly.

"Well, Anna girl, I've settled up everything so you can start clear and straight next Tuesday."

"Thank you, father. That will be grand."

There was a slight pause. Then Murphy said: "And your birthday is on Monday. It will be a great day, Anna girl. Do you feel excited about it all?"

"No," she said quietly, "I've got quite used to the idea. Father, are you going to give me anything for my birthday?"

"Of course, I am. Sure, why shouldn't I? It will be a great day for us both."

"What will it be?" she asked gravely.

"Now, wouldn't you rather a surprise, Anna? Something you wouldn't be knowing about beforehand?"

"No. I don't like surprises. They're never what you want."

"Well, then," he said proudly, "I'm going to give you a fine white dress. It's that covered with flounces you couldn't stick another one on anywhere. There's a grand pink sash to tie round your waist, and short sleeves with lace on. It's that long you'll have to be holding the skirt of it up, the way it won't be picking the mud up off the road, and you going to a party. I got it from Noonan's store, and there's a pair of silk stockings along with it, with lace all up the front. Noonan says they call it open-work. You won't see the like of them stockings anywhere in this town, except on your own two feet."

Johnny had listened with awe to the description of the princely gift. In his imagination, he had already clothed Anna in it, and was lost in admiration at the "open-work" silk stockings on her shapely ankles.

But the girl's voice sounded discontented.

"Have you bought the dress, father?" she was asking.

"I have not then. I was talking it over with Noonan yesterday." "Well, father"—she hesitated a second—"father, I wonder if you could give me the money you were going to spend on the dress, instead of the dress itself?"

Johnny gave a little gasp of surprise and disappointment. So did Murphy.

"Why, Anna, don't you want the dress?"

"Well, you see, father, I wouldn't hardly wear it. We don't go to parties, and you don't know what it would be ironing out those flounces. Besides, I've got enough dresses. The money would be more useful."

"But it's got blue ribbons and bones in the bodice of it," he pleaded. "I'll give you a hat with feathers on, too. I'd like to see you dressed up like a grand lady, Anna girl."

"I'd rather have the money, father."

Johnny heard James Murphy sigh.

"Well, Anna, it's your birthday. You must have what you like. That dress was a big price. Near five pounds I was going to give Noonan for it. I'll make it up to five pounds for you, if that will please you."

"Thank you ever so much, father."

They came out into the garden, where Johnny was still at the tap.

Murphy glared at him, but he addressed himself boldly to Anna.

"Miss Anna, could you spare me a lick of paint, if so be you have any in the house?"

She smiled at him, and his heart gave a bound in his side.

"You'll find some in the shed where the tools are kept," she said. "Lots of different colours. I forgot now what we used to use them for. Why do you want them?"

"For—for painting something, Miss Anna."

He retired hastily to the lobelia bed, and James Murphy scowled.

"I don't trust that fellow. I wish you'd get rid of him, Anna."

"Oh, there's nothing wrong with him," she said.

For the next few days Johnny was very busy up in his room. He told Anna he was mending the kitchen table there, but it seemed to her that he took a very long time over it.

When she took her sewing into the garden, she missed the tall, lean figure working among the flowers, and the haunting, eager voice that she liked to listen to. Sometimes when she sat there waiting for him in vain, she felt very lonely, as if he were a hundred miles away.

On the evening before her birthday, James Murphy came out to her, as she sewed on the bench outside the door.

"You're not looking happy, Anna."

"Aren't I?" she said listlessly.

"Anything the matter?"

"No, father, nothing."

He studied her grave, downcast face for a few moments.

"The day after to-morrow you'll be taking everything into your own hands," he said presently.

"Yes, father."

"I've told Breenan he can go. You said you wouldn't be wanting him."

She sighed.

"Thank you, father."

He tried to make her laugh.

"I'm thinking I ought to scratch my name off of the shop, and put 'A. Murphy' instead in big, gold letters. I could get Duffey to do it cheap."

She did not reply, and he bent down and looked at her anxiously.

"Anna, why is it you don't be talking about the shop near as much these days? Is there anything ails you?"

She got up and put her sewing into her basket.

"I'm all right, father," she said crossly. "Maybe I'm tired to-day."

Anna's birthday dawned fair and bright. There were sausages for breakfast, fried potatoes in bacon fat, and a jug of cream in honour of the event.

Anna brought in the sausages, wiped her hands on her apron and stood very straight, in anticipation of something she did not like. Her father walked slowly across the room, put his arms round her, and gave her a loud kiss in the middle of her cheek. She allowed him to do this, once every year. When it was over, she wiped the mark of the kiss with a corner of her apron, and said: "Good morning, father."

"Happy birthday, Anna. Here's your five pounds."

He handed her five rather dirty notes, and she took them eagerly.

"Thank you so much, father dear. Do you mind waiting on your tea while I go and lock them up?"

When she came back he was eating sausages with an appetite.

"Anna, I'm after hiring Clancy's jaunting car for the day. We'll go out into the country and bring food. Maybe you'd like the Gillians and Mat Cave to come along with us."

For a moment her face fell. Then she laughed, apparently at nothing.

"That will be fine, father. I'll go and see about the meals."

But she did not go to the kitchen. Instead, she pushed open the side door and walked into the garden.

Johnny was waiting for her with a brown paper parcel in his arms.

"Miss Anna"—a shy colour had come into his face and his eyes were appealing—"Miss Anna, it's your birthday, and I'm after making something for you. Maybe now you won't like it." He held the parcel out to her and she took it wonderingly from his hands.

"Johnny, you shouldn't have done this"; but she was opening it with eager, fumbling fingers. Inside was a wooden box, cut rudely in the shape of a heart. It was painted black, and there were fantastic scrolls and lines done on it in scarlet and blue and yellow. The effect was odd, but it was the most attractive thing she had ever seen. Johnny had been watching her face in an agony, but now a great, satisfied delight shone in his eyes.

"Will you open it, Miss Anna?" he urged.

She lifted the lid.

The inside of the box was the plain white wood, but a delicious lavender scent met her nostrils as she looked in.

"I picked some lavender heads," explained Johnny, "and soaked them in water. Then I put the water in the box and it soaked into the wood. 'Twas my mother taught me to make lavender water, when I was no more than a wee gossure living in Enniskerry."

Anna found words.

"It's lovely, Johnny. You are ever so clever to make such a beautiful thing. I've never had anything I liked so much. Wait now till I put it up in my room. I'm going to keep all my ribbons and handkerchiefs in it."

A light blazed up in his eyes. He started forward, and opened his lips.

"Anna!" James Murphy called from the top of the house.

"Coming, father. Johnny, thank you, thank you. I'll see you again in the evening."

She ran indoors, and met James Murphy in the passage.

"What's that you're carrying?" he said.

Anna was fundamentally, absolutely honest. She told the truth as naturally as some people tell lies. Indeed she was not able to invent a lie on the spur of the moment, even if she wished to.

"Johnny made it for my birthday, father," she said, displaying the box for his inspection.

"That fellow out there! Your birthday!" Murphy grew purple, and his laboured breath could hardly form the words. "The damned, unholy impudence of him! He deserves to be flogged."

"Father, what's come to you at all?" Some of Anna's views had changed so completely during the past few weeks that she could not understand his fury.

"I'll go out this very minute and give him the richest skelping he's ever had. The likes of him setting up to be giving you a present on your birthday!"

"I don't suppose you'd be able to flog him," she said rather scornfully. That inflamed him to madness.

"You wait and see what I'll do to him. As for that rubbish, give it here and I'll throw it into the kitchen fire. I'm surprised at you taking it from him."

He tried to wrench the box out of her hands, but she clung to it with all her strength.

"Leave go of it, father. How dare you do like this? It's not yours." A heavy coil of her hair had shaken loose and hung on her shoulder. Her face was flaming and defiant. "Oh, you're breaking it!" she cried. "If you break it, father, I'll tear your eyes out."

She burst into a sudden flood of tears, and he let go his grip on the box, feeling contrite and a little afraid.

"There, you may keep the box, Anna girl," he soothed. "I didn't mean to upset you." He put a clumsy arm round her shoulders.

"Do you know," he whispered, "this is the first time I've ever seen you cry."

Chapter VIII

The sun had gone down, and it was twilight-time.

The rich scent of the flowers asleep hung in the air and the drone of a hurdy-gurdy sounded faintly, far down the road.

Anna closed the door of the back parlour and stepped into the garden. She was very hot, and the breeze calmed and soothed her.

A dark figure arose from among the geraniums and hurried towards her.

"Miss Anna, is it yourself?"

She turned her head.

"Isn't it a nice evening, Johnny."

They leaned together on the gate and watched the stars glimmer out one by one.

"There's a cold wind," she said. "I think it's going to rain to-morrow."

"This morning I thought it would be better for me to be going away from here," said Johnny, staring up at the sky.

"Go away?" She caught her breath in a little gasp.

"But I thought this morning I wouldn't yet," he said, still keeping his eyes turned from her.

"Oh! what made you decide that?"

"I heard you and your father talking this morning about my box."

"Oh!" She grew a little annoyed.

At last he turned to her, and suddenly swept her into his arms.

"You love me, you love me! I knew it when I heard you crying, and it's the truth."

She panted and struggled a little.

"Let me go, Johnny. You're making me frightened."

He kissed her lips and her cheeks and her hair.

Then he let her go, and she gave a gasping little laugh.

"I loved you the first time I seen you leaning over the gate," he said huskily. "And you knew it all the time. Didn't you know it?"

He stretched hungry arms towards her again.

"Say you love me, Anna. Won't you be giving me one kiss?"

She put out her hands as if to ward him off.

"Don't hug me again, Johnny. I don't like it. Yes, I'll kiss you just once."

She bent forward, put her hands under his chin and kissed him on the mouth.

Johnny broke his promise.

He seized her again in his arms and held her with such mad, desperate strength that she screamed. Then he slipped on to the ground at her feet, kissing her shoes, crooning crazy, incoherent things.

Anna had never seen passion of any kind before. She scarcely knew what the word meant. Now she was frightened, and she shook him roughly by the shoulder.

"Johnny, get up, get up. What are you behaving like this mad, fool way for?"

He did not move. She touched his bowed head with her foot.

"Johnny, if you aren't sensible, I'll go in."

That brought him to his feet, with earth clinging to his hair and clothes.

She took his hands and pulled him across to the bench.

"Now we'll sit here," she said, "and talk it all over."

"Talk! I don't want to talk. I want just to be looking at you and kissing the face of you and your beautiful black hair. Won't you let down your hair, Anna, darling?"

In spite of herself, she liked his admiration. She took out the hairpins, and the rippling mass uncoiled itself and fell like a curtain over her shoulders.

She watched him take a few strands reverently in his fingers and stroke them.

Then she said patiently:

"We must talk things over, Johnny. It's going to be very hard."

He was a little amazed at her calm acceptance of the situation, and her readiness to discuss cold facts. He had not yet got over the stupendous fact of their love.

"Sure it's not hard at all," he contradicted. "We love each other, and that's all there is to it."

She kicked the ground impatiently.

"You are foolish, Johnny. Father will be like a mad bull with rage when we tell him. I don't know how we'll manage about him."

"Is it telling Mr. Murphy you'll be?" he asked in amazement.

"Of course, Johnny. What did you think?"

Under her clear eyes, he flushed a slow red. "I was thinking we'd run away out of this, the two of us, and he wouldn't know about it at all."

She experienced a slight shock of disappointment in him.

"Oh, no, Johnny," she said briskly, "we mustn't do that. You see, the right thing is to tell him, and I always like to try the right thing first, even if I have to do the wrong one afterwards. Besides, it would be, cowardly just to run away like that!"

"That's a true word and no lie," admitted Johnny, feeling a little ashamed. "But if he says no, what will you do then?"

She sat up very straight, and a wonderful strength and purpose came into her face.

"If he says no, I'll run away with you, Johnny. You see," she leaned towards him, "I love you so very much, I'll always stick to you whatever happens."

He put out his arms again, but he arrested himself and instead lifted a long lock of her hair to his lips.

"You see," she began after a little pause, "father may be very angry, Johnny. He never liked you, and he may send you away when he hears about this. So perhaps I won't see you at all to-morrow. But I'll tell you now what you must do. Now listen, Johnny. Leave my hair alone," she jerked the heavy mane out of his grasp. "You must arrange with Father Conolly—he's the parish priest and a nice old man, so he is—for us to be married in the chapel tomorrow night. I'll get some people to be witnesses. Do you understand, Johnny?"

She had explained this very much as she had explained to him the work he was to do in the garden and, as he listened, his face grew rather blank.

"You haven't listened," she said irritably.

"I have, then. Admiring the way you speak, I was. One would think you're after planning the whole of it out in your head beforehand, so they would."

He was nearer the truth than he knew, but the truth made her feel a little ashamed.

Suddenly he put his arm round her again and drew her close to him.

"I was longing and longing to do this since the day I saw you first," he whispered. "Oh, Anna, isn't it wonderful that you love me back?"

"Why is it so wonderful?" She gave a little laugh.

"You speak different to me, and all. You're a real lady, Anna, so you are."

"Oh, I'm not," she protested. "Father gave me a good schooling, and we've never mixed with the people in this town, but I've seen real grand ladies drive past in their carriages, with four horses sometimes and a coachman set up so proud and fine, and I'm not like them. I don't think," reflectively, "that I want to be."

"Darling!" he crooned. "Anna, darling, kiss me."

"I have once."

"But you love me. Don't you want to be kissing me like I feel about you?"

Firmly she plucked his clinging hands off her shoulders.

"I don't hold with kissing," she said. "Can't you believe I love you without me messing over you all the time?"

"Anna girl—"

"I can't explain, Johnny, but I love something inside you that isn't you at all, not the body part of you. Don't you feel the same?"

He shook his head and stared at her with great, puzzled eyes.

"But you're so beautiful, Anna. Maybe you feel that way because I'm—not beautiful."

She studied his face for a moment. She knew that most people would have called it a beautiful face, the face of a dreamer, a poet and idealist. Then she turned her head away and looked out at the garden and the rising moon.

"There's the question of money," she said slowly.

"How can you be talking about money and the like of that?"

"Oh, Johnny," she sighed, "don't you see we must talk reasonably if we are in earnest over this? Let me see. I have twenty-five pounds saved up, counting the five pounds father gave me. That should do until we can find work. We shall have to work, Johnny, won't we?"

He had buried his hands in her hair and was entangling them adoringly in its soft, heavy coils.

He tried to follow her in her rapid vibrations between love and business, but he could not do it, and she had to answer for him.

"I know you don't like work, Johnny. If I hadn't been so fond of you, I would have been very angry at the way you kept pulling off the heads of the weeds and leaving the roots in the ground. What can you do to earn money, Johnny?"

"Och, there's time enough to talk of them things," he murmured, pressing his lips on the top of her head. He was shabby, but he smelt of tobacco and clean things, and she did not recoil from him.

"You must plan ahead, if you want to get on," she said. "Oh, Johnny, Johnny, don't you see it's just because I love you so very much that I'm making these schemes for us? I want you to get work so we can be so happy together, not poor and hungry like you were when you first came here. We had better go right away up to Dublin. We'll find something there."

"Anna, darling," he whispered, "tell me what made you love me first. There's great wonder in that, so there is."

"Oh, I don't know. I don't see how anybody can really know that. I was not sure that I did care for you, till father tried to take that box from me. Johnny, it's getting so late, I must go in to father. But, as you didn't listen last time, I'd best tell you again what you must do to-morrow if father sends you out of the house and we don't see each other."

She explained again, and he made an effort to drag his thoughts from her hair and her sunburnt throat, and listen intelligently.

"Is it marriage that's in it?" he asked in a puzzled voice, as she finished speaking.

"What do you mean?" she said sharply.

"Nothing at all," he said, "but I was thinking we might run now and get married in Dublin, the way we'd save time if Mr. Murphy maybe was out after us."

He got a shocked look from her honest eyes.

"Johnny, I couldn't run away with you if we were not married. It would be wrong."

"Well, disobeying your father, and him angry mad with you, that's wrong too, I'm thinking."

"It's wrong," she said reflectively, "but I think it would be more—legal. Besides, if we did what you want, think what people would say."

He stared at her incredulously.

"Anna, you'd not mind what Tim Johnson and the like of him do be saying about you? Sure it wouldn't matter a *poreen* to us, would it?"

"Of course I would mind," she said. "Why, Johnny, it matters just everything, what people think of you. If you aren't going to care what they say, I don't see how you're going to get on."

She rose from the bench and began to fasten up her hair.

"You're not leaving me?" Johnny asked longingly.

"I must. I want to tell father all about it. Then he can sleep on it and perhaps he'll think better of it in the morning. Perhaps, perhaps, Johnny, he won't mind it so very much. Wouldn't that be grand!"

"I'll not let you tell him," he protested. "Sure amn't I the one who ought to be doing all the dirty work? Let you wait here while I speak to him."

He had risen eagerly, but she pushed him back.

"No, Johnny, I could do it best. I'm not afraid of father. I'll be a proud woman, standing up, telling him I love you. I will, so."

All flushed, and bright-eyed and self-confident, she bent and touched his forehead with her lips.

"Good night, Johnny."

"Good night," he whispered, clinging to her. "May God keep you safe till morning."

Chapter IX

Anna came in from the garden and stood for a moment outside the parlour door. Then she pushed it open and walked in.

James Murphy sat in the armchair, smoking his pipe and gazing with lazy contentment at the picture of Anna's mother which hung opposite him in a gilt frame. The face was a little like Anna's, with the hardness of mouth and chin left out.

He looked up as the girl came in and noted her flushed checks and the brightness in her eyes.

"Well, Anna girl, you look excited over something."

"Do I, father? I've been out in the garden." She leant against the mantelpiece, gazing at the window as if she hoped to see something out there in the dark.

"Are you after having a good time on your birthday, Anna?" he questioned fondly.

"Oh, father, such a wonderful time. I don't think I've ever had such a grand birthday in my life."

"Well, I'm glad of that," he said, "and tomorrow you'll be taking over the shop, and I'll be sitting here smoking my old pipe, and admiring the way you'll be managing things. You that were a wee girleen not so long ago. Playing with coloured bricks you'd be, and your mother and I watching you and laughing. I used to be taking you on my knee the way you could play with my watch-chain. Well,

well, it's a fine woman you're grown, Anna, so you are."

His words kindled no enthusiasm in her face, though he looked anxiously for it.

"Why have you three candles burning, father?" she said. "You know we never have more than two in summer." She blew one of the candles out, and her face seemed to disappear into shadow.

"Well, it's getting late," he said. "I was going to my bed, anyway."

He rose heavily and stretched his arms above his head.

"Father!" she said.

"Well, Anna girl, what is it?"

"I have something to tell you."

Her voice did not quiver, but he sensed the strong excitement underlying it.

"What is it?" he repeated uneasily.

"Father, I am going to be married."

He swung round and stared at her.

"What? What are you saying at all?" Fear had come into his eyes, but suddenly they grew normal again and he laughed. "Well, Anna, you thought this was a great surprise, but I can tell you I knew it all along. Oh, I saw it coming so I did, and I'm glad, I'm real glad about it. Kiss me, Anna, and tell me all about it."

She drew back from him in amazement.

"Father," she faltered, "did you say you were *glad*?"

"And why wouldn't I be indeed? A nice, honest, decent lad he is and his father before him. Well, he's waited for you long enough, and I'm glad you listened to him at the last."

"What do you mean?" she cried.

"Isn't it Mat Cave that's in it? I watched him to-day and he sitting foreninst you in the jaunting car. I thought to myself the way it would end."

He began to chuckle quietly, hut her voice cut sharply across his merriment.

"Father, I don't know what you mean. I scarcely spoke two words to Mat Cave the whole of this day."

He stared dumbly at her and she braced herself to deliver the shock.

"I'm going to be married to Johnny Croghan," she said.

For a second there was silence in the room. Then James Murphy burst out laughing again, but this time with distorted mouth and a strange hint of disaster in his laughter.

"You're funning, Anna," he burbled. "It's a joke you're having on me."

She came to him out of the shadow, the hard lines round her mouth drawn and emphasised.

"Stop laughing, father," she ordered. "Can't you see, can't you see I'm serious? Johnny Croghan asked me to marry him not ten minutes ago, and"—she paused an instant—"I said yes."

He looked up and saw that she was serious indeed. Her eyes were deeply earnest, her voice shook with the intensity of her declaration. He tried to disbelieve, but looking at her and listening to her, he could not do it.

"It's nonsense you're talking," he said sulkily. "Johnny Croghan is a tramp, an outcast. There's great shame on you for daring to speak about him this way."

"You don't understand, father," she broke in. "I tell you I love Johnny. It is not a fancy; it will last for always, all my whole life. I love him, and I'm going to marry him. There's no shame in that."

"He's got a face like them holy pictures in Steenan's window, that's why. You think you're serious, my girl, hut you don't understand what you're saying."

"Father, how can you talk like that? I'm not a child." She bit her lips, for his contemptuous tone hurt her and made her angry.

"You're a little fool," flashed James Murphy.

"I was a fool to have told you."

She began to walk to the door, but he called her back.

"Anna, where are you going?"

"I'm going upstairs. There's no use talking to you. You won't be sensible."

The unflinching purpose of her eyes and mouth frightened him. He began to fight desperately.

"Think of the shop, Anna. You wouldn't be leaving the shop and you just going to take over the whole of it?"

The laugh she gave seemed to be wrung out of her forcibly.

"The shop! Oh, father, what a fool you are! I wouldn't care if the shop and everything in it was blown to smithereens this very moment."

He knew she was speaking the truth. He did not plead "Think of me," for he knew that would not prevail against her.

He had sensed something of her divine selfishness, her indifference in this supreme moment, to all his hopes and plans for her, his despair and humiliation.

"To think of the two of you making love under my nose and me as innocent and unsuspicious as a two-year-old child," he raged.

"We didn't make love," said Anna. "He never said a word to me till this morning. And, father, we've done the right thing, coming and telling you. We want you to consent, but, of course, if you won't—"

"Consent!" he shouted. "What are you talking about?"

"Then, father, we'll get married without it. I'm being quite honest with you, you see."

"I'll send that impudent blackguard away. Out of the house he goes this very night. God Almighty, if I could have guessed—"

"You see now," she said, "that I mean what I say."

"I'll lock you into your room all to-morrow, so you can't run after him."

"You can do that, father." Her face was hardened into lines of iron resolution. He saw it, and suddenly a realisation of all she meant to him swept over him.

"Anna, Anna, you can't mean it. Do forget all about it and be sensible again."

She did not answer, and he came close to her.

"It's not like you at all, Anna. You so clever and sensible and level-headed. You'd never do the like of this. I'll not believe you're serious, not if you tell me so a thousand times. I'll not, so."

"I won't trouble to tell you more than the once," she said.

"Well, Anna, tell me what made you feel like that about him. Just tell me that."

"Oh, I couldn't. I could never explain that to you. But, father," her voice deepened with determination, "let me tell you this. You may send Johnny away, and lock me up, but we'll get married somehow. I love Johnny, and I'll stick to him always, and nothing you do will make any difference to that."

"You wouldn't run away, Anna," he whispered; "you wouldn't do that on me."

"Yes, I would," she said hardly, "if there was no other way."

"You little fool! You think you could live on nothing while you're tramping the roads. How are you going to live?"

"I've got twenty-five pounds saved up of my own," she defended herself. "That will keep us till we get work."

"You don't know what you're saying," he stormed. "What do you know about work?" He looked up and saw her inexorable eyes, the lines round the stern, young mouth. "Oh, there's no use in arguing with you," he cried.

He knew she had beaten him, and his defeat made him brutal with fury.

"I'll send that scoundrel packing this very moment," he threatened. "Not another night will he sleep under this roof. I'll thrash the liver out of him, the blackguard. Maybe it's only playing he was with you. You were silly and didn't know anything. Maybe he was amused—"

Anna caught him by the arm.

"Father, stop that at once. Oh, how can you!"

"If I thought it," said James Murphy, "I'd flog the guts out of him. I'd flay him alive." He went out of the room, and Anna heard his heavy steps echoing along the passage.

Johnny had not left the garden. He stood leaning over the gate watching the moon flinging its beams across the housetops opposite him. He heard a step on the grass and turned round with a sudden hope.

But it was James Murphy who was tramping towards him, each foot falling heavily as if it were an effort for him to lift them.

Johnny did not move until he came near.

Then he said: "It's a fine evening," because he could think of nothing else.

"You've got to get out of this," said James Murphy through his clenched teeth. He was breathing thickly as though he had been running.

"Get out?" repeated Johnny.

Then Murphy's sorrow and fury broke out of bounds. He began

to curse Johnny in a low voice that gradually rose to a pinnacle of raging vehemence, and then sank again to a hoarse whisper.

Johnny made no retort. He glimpsed the tragedy behind the man's florid face and abusive words. Standing there in the moonlight, James Murphy looked much older and weaker. His hair was nearly white and his hands were shaking as he clenched them.

When he turned his back to Johnny and fought for control, Johnny felt for him a little of the pity that had not occurred to Anna. He was beaten. What could he do with youth and love in league against him?

Murphy turned, and the moonlight showed him the pity in Johnny's eyes.

"You've got to clear out of this to-night," he said venomously, "you—" The words that followed brought a faint red to Johnny's face. But an innate chivalry told him to be gentle with a fallen foe, and he answered quite quietly:

"I won't sleep here to-night. I'll be going to my room now and taking away a few things with me."

His submission gained him a quick glance of contempt from Murphy's eyes.

Then the old man turned and went slowly back to the house, his feet falling this time with strange unsteadiness on the grass.

Chapter X

At seven o'clock the next evening, Anna and Johnny were married. Mat Cave and a girl friend of Anna's were the amazed witnesses. Mat watched the ceremony with sullen bitterness, and the girl with wild excitement and envy of the romance.

The priest was also a little surprised, and read the service dubiously.

"It isn't the kind of wedding I'd planned to have," whispered Anna to her husband as they came out of the church, "but it was nicer. Don't you feel very happy, Johnny?"

She was wearing a white dress and a hat with blue ribbons. The buckles on her shoes glistened in the last rays of the sunset. "I couldn't wear a wedding gown," she explained to Johnny, "but I put on my best. Do you like it?"

For answer he drew her close to him and kissed her radiant cheeks.

"Don't, don't!" she cautioned. "Everyone on the road will see us."

"Let them!" he said recklessly. "It doesn't matter that brass ring if everyone in Ireland does be looking at us. You're mine now, Anna, and I'm so happy I could be capering and cutting the buckle all along the road better than the dancing-master himself, if so be they wouldn't have me up as a mad-creature because of it."

Anna drew herself a little away from him.

"When you say 'that brass ring,'" she said, with an attempt at coldness, "I expect you mean my wedding ring. You put it on my finger in the church because we hadn't another, you know, though goodness knows where you got it from."

"Never mind that," he said uncomfortably; "but I didn't mean you to be wearing it afterwards. You'd best take it off of your finger, Anna. Them things bring no luck."

She glanced at her third finger round which hung a thick brass ring. Johnny had taken it from his pocket during the ceremony, and she recalled the curious hesitation with which he had placed it on her finger. Suddenly, the vision of an open sack came before her eyes, with leather straps in it, and a rope coiled up. There had been a brass ring on the end of that rope.

Without quite knowing why she did it, she plucked the ring off her finger and threw it on the ground.

"It is too big," she said, "and it doesn't really matter about a ring. Why, Johnny, what are you picking it up for?"

"Maybe I'll want it," he muttered. "I wouldn't like to be leaving it there."

"Oh, Johnny," she cried, "you're still carrying that sack. Whatever can you want with it?"

He gave her a sharp glance and answered in a low voice:

"There's things in it I couldn't do without."

They had been walking along the road that led out of the village. Anna never once looked behind. There was a gay light in her eyes as they moved farther and farther away. She would not let Johnny carry the new paper parcel in which she had stowed her belongings, but carried it easily under one arm.

"We shall sleep to-night at Nolan's Inn," she told him, "then we'll walk to the station and catch the train to Dublin."

"Are you certain, then, your father wouldn't forgive you if we stayed in the town!" he questioned.

"Father," she said reflectively, "is weak in places and strong in places. He might forgive me, but he'd want me to come back and live with him. He would never, never have you near him again, so it would be hard to live in the town and hear the neighbours talking, and father wouldn't speak to me so long as I went on living with you. So we'll get right away, and perhaps one day—" She paused, for her limited imagination could not realise a time when James Murphy might have reconciled himself to hearing her called Mrs. Johnny Croghan. There was no regret in her voice as she spoke of her father's hostility. She lived entirely in the present, except when she considered the meals for to-morrow. That was her only peep into the future.

As they walked along, Johnny put his arm round her. Her nearness gave him such ecstasies of joy that he felt quite dazed. The sunset faded off the sky, and a hushed twilight came down.

"Oh," said Anna suddenly, "I wish we had more money. I've suddenly realised twenty-five pounds is so little, Johnny; what shall we do if there's no work for us in Dublin?"

The pessimism was so unlike her that it made him feel something must have happened to her. But he loved the idea of protecting her, so he said soothingly:

"Sure, what's come to you, Anna, agra? Are you afraid of coming away alone with me?"

"Oh, no, no!"

"Didn't I promise I'd get work for you? I'll be making your twenty-five pounds up to fifty before you know where you are."

She smiled as she would at a boastful child.

"I tell you, I can earn money," he cried hotly. "Sure there isn't a job in the whole of the world I wouldn't be glad to do for you, Anna, so there isn't. Is it laughing you are?"

"I can't help it, Johnny. You get so worked up, it's funny."

"All right," he said, mortified by her tone, "but you wait till you see the half-crowns and the five shilling bits I'll be bringing home to you soon."

They walked on in silence till a bend in the road revealed a long, low house, with a sign swinging over the door.

"This is Nolan's," said Anna. "I've heard father say, many a time, it's a respectable place. Still, you never know."

She hung back a little as they entered, for she had never slept outside her bedroom over the grocer's shop.

"Come on," said Johnny. "We'll have to sleep here, respectable or not respectable, for there's no place else for us."

"You don't really know what respectable is, do you, Johnny," remarked Anna, more as if stating a regrettable fact than asking a question.

"Sure I do." He was up in arms. "I call this house respectable. It's a grand house, fit for a lord."

He asked for a double room, and they secured one of dubious cleanliness, with a huge curtained bed standing in the centre.

The man, Nolan, accompanied them into the room and enlarged eloquently on the glories of the bed. It was his great-grandmother's bed, the best in the house. He pointed proudly to the carved cherubs climbing among the leaves and scrolls on the gilt posts of it. The curtains were green and moth-eaten, but they could not take away from the beauty of the bed. It stood out grandly from among the scanty, squalid furniture.

Anna blushed hotly as the description went on.

"Do tell him to go," she whispered to Johnny.

"It's a grand wedding bed for us," said Johnny when they were alone, "only the curtains are green. That means no luck to us. I wouldn't like to be sleeping between green curtains."

"Oh, Johnny," she sighed, "I wish you were not so superstitious."

He did not answer, but he turned sullenly away and she saw the ashamed colour steal into his face.

"Oh, I'm tired," said Anna, "Johnny, I think I'll just get into bed and go to sleep."

"Won't you be wanting your supper then?"

"I'm not very hungry."

She began to fidget about the room and Johnny sat on the bed, wondering why she did not begin to take off her clothes.

Presently she came towards him.

"Johnny, I want to undress."

"What is there preventing you?" he said.

Anna glanced at the door, blushing again.

"Johnny, will you—do you mind?"

His eyes were amazed and hurt.

"Just till I get used to being married," she pleaded, the tears coming into her eyes. "With you in the room I feel I can't—"

Johnny got up without a word and walked to the door, not understanding her in the least, and feeling absurdly miserable.

Anna watched him go out, then undressed rapidly and blew out the candle. She knelt down by the bed and prayed God to make her a good wife and to let them he happy. Then she crept into the blankets and drew them over her.

In that unfamiliar room, she found herself wondering at the impulse and bravery that had brought her there. It was the first impulsive thing she had ever done in her life, and now that it was all over, she could scarcely believe that it was she who had done it.

But for Johnny, darling, queer Johnny, she would do it again a thousand times.

All her love for him surged up inside her like a huge balloon, making her feel very light and happy. She buried her head in the pillow and prayed again to be a useful, dutiful wife.

Downstairs, Johnny leaned on the mantelpiece trying to beat down this first bitter disappointment. He could not understand Anna's viewpoint at all. The only solution that presented itself to his untutored mind was that she was afraid of him. His delicate sense of chivalry was hurt and insulted. The room he stood in was a large one, illuminated by the smoky flare of two lamps. At one end a table had been placed and five men, evidently habitués, were gathering round it for cards.

One of them stared hard at Johnny. Then he came up to him.

"I'm thinking I know the face of you," he said doubtfully. Johnny turned sullenly away.

"Maybe I'm mistook," said the man, a little surprised. "But leaving that question, I'm here to ask if you'll join in with us for vanjohn. We're wanting a sixth, and you'll make us complete."

Johnny hesitated before the friendliness of the invitation.

"I will not then," he refused, but not very resolutely.

"Arrah, talk sense," said the man persuasively. "You've a lucky face on you."

"Divil a bit of luck I ever have at cards, or at anything else."

"Now why wouldn't you have the luck with you to-night?" tempted the man. "Once I saw a gossure with sixpence in his pocket win five pounds in a night, and he with a lucky face on him like you. I minded him when you come in, so I did."

A flame had suddenly leaped up in Johnny's eyes. He had no money of his own, but what if he gambled with Anna's little hoard and added five pounds to it, for her? Anna's doubts of his ability to earn a living had wounded the manhood in him.

"I'll play with you," he said briefly to the man. "Wait now till I get a few pounds I have above there."

He raced exultantly up the stairs and into their room.

Anna lay asleep in the magnificent bed. Her face was a little flushed, and her hair was braided into a neat plait.

Johnny leaned over her for a few moments in silent worship. Then he kissed the rounded arm that peeped above the blankets, very lightly, for fear he should wake her.

He found the money locked away in a purse she usually wore round her waist, and took fifteen pounds. It must be realised that he did not care for cards. He was doing this simply and solely for Anna's sake. She had said that she wished they had more than twenty-five pounds on which to start their married life, and he was granting her wish, thinking already of the delight her joy and gratitude would give him.

He went downstairs and was hailed merrily by the five men. They all seemed amazingly well supplied with cash and the play was rather high.

Johnny was diffident and nervous at first. Then, as he won steadily, he became reckless. The little pile of money beside him grew bigger. Johnny was thrilled and amazed at his good luck. Anna would never dare to doubt him again. The gambling fire ran riot in his blood, and at midnight he dashed upstairs to get the remaining ten pounds so that he could make it into twenty.

After this he lost a few times, but it only increased his eager excitement.

Recklessly he began to bet higher and higher. He lost more often. In two hours he only won three times.

"Your luck's giving out," one of the men remarked.

"It is so," admitted Johnny. He was getting a little frightened. "Maybe I'll not play anymore," he suggested.

"You'll not be leaving us yet, Mr. Croghan," they protested. "You want to win it all back again. You'll be winning again if you stick to it, so you will."

So Johnny stuck to it, and lost steadily. Despair entered into him, like a cold finger suddenly laid on his heart. "I haven't the twenty-five pounds left to me now," he whispered.

But he still fought desperately, and hopelessly. The little pile of money beside him ebbed slowly away.

During a pause in the game, he counted it surreptitiously, and a sort of sick horror paralysed his limbs for a second. There remained only four pounds and seven shillings.

He rose up, miserable and rather near tears.

"I'll not play another hand," he said fiercely. "You're after ruining me. There's great sorrow on me, I ever played with you at all."

They laughed at this, and Johnny's blood boiled. Their faces, half seen through the murky light, were mocking him.

As he dragged himself out of the room, one of the men whispered: "That fellow, has he all his wits, do you think?"

"I'm thinking I know his face well," said the one who had spoken to Johnny first. "I wouldn't say but he's a bit daft." They winked.

Johnny put the money back in his wife's purse. He undressed, and climbed wearily into bed. Anna woke up in the flare of the candle, and started a little at sight of him.

"Why are you so late?" she whispered.

"I was talking to them below there. Oh, I'm tired to death."

How should he tell her? How should he tell her?

* * * * * *

Johnny had intended to wake very early and do something with the money. Perhaps he would hide the purse, pretend it had been stolen.

He could have faced the truth bravely enough if Anna's respect for him had not been at stake. Anna would despise him and he could not bear it. Her anger and contempt haunted his dreams. He slept uneasily for much longer than he had meant to, and when he awoke it was to see Anna fully dressed, drawing back the green curtains.

"You're up," he murmured dazedly.

"Oh, Johnny, such an awful thing. We must have been robbed in the night. Every penny of our money gone except four pounds seven shillings! What *shall* we do?"

He stared at her, his lips and cheeks dead white.

"Johnny!" she cried. "What's the matter with you? Oh"—the blood rushed up to her neck, "Johnny, you can't know anything about it?"

He gulped down something in his throat.

"Don't ask me, Anna."

"Tell me the truth," she said. "Oh, Johnny, whatever you do don't tell me a lie."

"You'll hate me, Anna. You'll despise me. Och! I wish I was dead this minute."

In a moment her arms were round him; she was crooning over him, as if he had been a sick child.

"Tell me, Johnny, tell me. I won't be angry."

So he told her, very unsteadily, and she did not remove her arms.

Her caresses were so rare that even in his misery this thrilled him.

"That's how it was," he whispered at the conclusion. "Oh, Anna, it's a curse and a sorrow I'll be to you. You'll be sorry you ever married me."

"Well, it can't be helped," she said soothingly. "I know you did it for me. And don't talk that nonsense, Johnny. We'll be very happy yet."

She drew her arms from him, because the impulse that had prompted the embrace was gone from her.

Johnny longed to kiss her and to feel her near him again, but he was not worthy yet for that bliss, even though she had forgiven him.

"We'll just have to walk to Dublin," she said cheerily, "and trust to luck to find someone on the way that will give us our food. Dublin isn't very far." Her robust young mind had thrown off the tragedy of the money and was making plans for the future, while his was still miserably groping in the darkness of self-reproach and sorrow.

"Johnny," she said rather awkwardly, "don't ever tell me a lie. I'll always stand by you whatever you do. You mustn't be a coward."

"You say that now," said Johnny incredulously, "but I know there are some things you wouldn't forgive."

"Yes, I would. Anything except murder and stealing and telling lies—things that would disgrace us and people wouldn't speak to us for. And, Johnny, even if you tell a lie when you're caught suddenly"—she was unconsciously learning his character—"you can always come out with the truth afterwards. It's never too late to mend."

"Sometimes," said Johnny, "you can be too late, and there's times, too, when you'd be frightened to tell the truth, because of the dreadful things that would happen to you."

He was thinking of Job Moran.

Chapter XI

That was how it began—the most terrible two months of Johnny's life.

Afterwards he used to shudder when he looked back on them.

There was no work for himself and Anna on the way to Dublin. The cottages could not employ them, and the small houses would not employ them, and they did not dare to appeal to the big houses.

Anna's five pounds dwindled away like water soaking through sand.

She did not complain very much about this, but sometimes Johnny, seeing the despair forcing its way into her young eyes, would throw himself on the ground, almost mad with remorse and self-reproach.

Then she would say: "Get up, Johnny, and don't take on about what can't be helped. I have no patience with you when you get fooling."

And he would feel like killing himself.

Some of the houses were willing enough to give them food, but this Anna's middle-class pride could not endure.

"I wouldn't mind if the gentry offered us a bite now and again," she explained to Johnny, "but these people are no better than me—not as good, some of them—and I don't feel I can beg from them."

He did not understand her point of view in the least, but he accepted it as usual with reverence as something above his uneducated mind.

Anna, indeed, climbed down from her prejudice when she discovered that charity was their only hope of food, but houses were few and far between on the road they were travelling, and she often lay down at night with a gnawing pain at the pit of her stomach.

Every day they walked as far as they could, and slept in a sheltered spot when twilight came down.

"I shall have to sell my best frock and my other gingham," Anna said one day, as they trudged along. The parcel under her arm had grown smaller, for everything in it had been sold except the two frocks. "Johnny, isn't there anything at all you have that we could sell?"

Johnny clutched his bag closer to him. "There's nothing in here only rubbish," he said. "No one would be wanting the things I have in this bag."

Anna stumbled over a stone and nearly fell. Overhead there was a brazen sky and the heat was cruel.

"Darling, you're tired," said Johnny. "Let you sit down on this bank and I'll see if there's a crumb of bread left on me."

She sank down on the grass, and he bent over her, stroking her bowed head.

"Oh, Anna, I'm wondering how you can bear the like of this," he whispered. "Sorrow take the day I ever saw you, and you'd be sewing in your father's garden this very hour."

"I'm all right," she said. "I can put up with a lot, you know. I'm very strong."

He threw himself down beside her and put his face down on her hands.

"Anna, Anna, we'll start this minute and go back to your father. I'll put you back in the garden with the geraniums, though it would tear the heart out of my body. I have a pain to see you like this, you that was happy and beautiful—"

She felt hot tears on her hands, dropping through her fingers.

"Arrah, have sense," she scolded. "Isn't it a great shame to see a big man like you crying! Come on now and we'll see if there's a town near where I can sell these dresses."

"God bless you, Anna," he said brokenly. "There isn't your like in the whole world."

Two miles farther on they came to a tiny village, and Anna sold the mauve gingham for half a crown to the one miscellaneous little shop. Johnny was waiting for her when she came out.

"Hurroo!" he shouted. "We're just ten miles from Dublin. Come on, Anna, and we'll buy a celebration feast."

With one of his sudden transitions from mood to mood, he was wildly gay. His eyes shone and the colour flushed his face, making it quite beautiful. In his imprudent way, he bought slabs of cake and a bottle of peppermints. Anna, who could not forgive extravagance, stood by the counter in silence. When he asked her what she would have, she murmured something incoherent, and put her hand to her head.

"Have you a pain, darling?" he questioned anxiously.

"It's nothing," she said a little more steadily, and he was satisfied.

The money flew in Johnny's hands, so they could not sleep in the town.

Johnny selected a field just beyond it for their night's resting-place, and brought Anna and the provisions to it triumphantly.

"I'm cold," said Anna with a little shiver.

So he collected sticks and leaves and lit a fire. Then he began to unwrap his parcels. He had a sweet tooth, and the slices of cherry cake delighted his eyes.

"I don't feel hungry," said Anna faintly.

"Not hungry!" He was amazed and disappointed. "Try a peppermint, agra. I'm after buying them for I knew they were your favourite sweet things."

"No," she said; "take them away."

He crawled forward and looked closely at her. The firelight danced over her hair and her closed eyes. Her face was very white.

"Anna, Anna!" he whispered.

She did not answer.

"Och, she's going asleep," he said.

He placed his sack under her head, and lay down beside her, throwing his arm across her body.

All through his dreams he seemed to hear her moaning and talking to herself.

Once her voice sounded loudly in his ear.

"Come on, Johnny. We'll never get to Dublin at this rate. Oh!" with a little wail, "he's very good but he's so useless. There isn't a single thing he can do. There's no shame in him for that."

Johnny sat up and looked at her. The dying fire showed him her face, which was very still and haggard. For a moment he thought her eyes were open, then he saw the thick lashes on her cheeks.

"Anna!" he called. "Anna!"

She did not speak or move.

He shook her gently by the shoulder, and she rolled limply from side to side.

Then terror took hold of him and almost choked him. He lifted her lax body in his arms and began to stumble across the field. In the town they would give her a bed and some milk. His anxiety made him quite sick. If Anna died, he would eat that whole clump of deadly nightshade.

He prayed desperately: "Don't let her die. Don't let her die till I get to the town."

She grew heavier and heavier in his arms, and his breath came in laboured gasps. In his agony he gave a broken little cry and an owl answered it and flew past his face. At last he struggled on to the road which led through the village. He saw a light in front of him, a friendly light which escaped through a broken, dusty window-pane. A square house took shape in the darkness.

"Praise be to God," he muttered, "it's a pub."

A dirty woman listened sympathetically to his appeal for help.

"Angels and ministers of grace defend us, isn't it the terrible misfortune that's come to you," she said. "Your wife to get ill on you and you married only two months. Wait now till I look at her."

She bent down and examined Anna's face. Johnny still held her, and her hair, which had fallen down, flowed over his arm like a cloak.

"The poor creature is starved," said the woman. "Let you carry her upstairs now, and I'll put her to bed. Musha, musha, isn't it a sad thing to see a beautiful young lady in a state the like of this."

She glanced rather suspiciously at Johnny as she led the way up the dark, filthy stairs, but, seeing the tortured devotion in his eyes, the look changed to one of kindness.

They entered a small room, and she lit a candle stuck in a saucer of earth.

"You can lay her on the bed," she said tersely to Johnny. The bed was unclean and had not been made, for many days, but Johnny in his sanest moments would not have noticed this.

"It's my own bed," explained the woman, "and it's a soft bed. Now I'll look after the poor thing, and you go to the room below and take something."

Johnny hung longingly in the doorway, but she would not hear of his staying, and he wept slowly down the stairs.

"I'll be going now across the field to fetch my bag," he muttered to himself.

So he crept out of the house and wearily retraced his steps. The faint glow of the fire guided him, and he picked up Anna's parcel, and his own sack with the impress of her head still on it.

A drizzling rain was falling as he returned, and he was glad to go into the warm, lighted room, heavy with pipe smoke and fumes.

He sat down by the fire and listened idly to the talk of seven men who were responsible for the atmosphere.

"Did you see," said one who wore a matted beard, "that Macdonald and Reeves—God help them—were found guilty?"

"Condemned to death, they were," added another man, an eager-eyed fellow with bare feet.

"Macdonald that was as innocent of that murder as my own childer beyond there," lamented the first speaker.

"What way is it you're talking, Joe Duveen"—it was another voice—"you that have no knowledge of the case at all—"

"Let you shut your ugly mouth, if you're not wanting it done for you," shouted the eager youth.

"Will you leave off talking of mouths, Jamesy Canavan, and you with one on you that could swallow a hen the way it does be hanging open."

The bearded man's melancholy voice filled the pause. "It's a great shame the way the law does be grinding us down. But sure there's no justice or mercy in this country, nor there won't be till we get the guiding of it into our own hands."

Johnny listened dreamily to the heated political argument that followed.

He was thinking of Macdonald and Reeves. The names of those two convicts had awakened so many memories. The atmosphere of prisons was round him again. The official faces of governors and under-sheriffs rose up before him.

He could smell the air of stuffy second-class railway carriages, and the stations where a hostile crowd used to wait for him.

Under his feet was the sack where his pinioning straps and his rope were. They revived a faint longing for the rising at grey dawn, the final preparations in the scaffold house, the walk through dim passages to the cell where the condemned man waited with the chaplain. He remembered the painful thrill that always seized him on the scaffold as he began to fasten the leg straps. It used to make his hands shake a little when he drew the lever. The longing changed to a vague regret. He was under the morbid fascination criminology exercises over certain minds.

He roused himself with difficulty, and listened to the conversation of the seven men.

"They say Moore had to resign," Joe Duveen was saying. "There's no wonder in that. He was not made for the job."

"Who is this you're talking about?" asked Johnny shyly, trying to take an interest.

There was a sudden silence as the men turned to look at him.

"Who would it be but Pete Moore," volunteered the barefooted youth; "he that was hangman after Cregan resigned. 'Hanging Johnny' they called that one in his own place, I've heard."

"And is Moore resigning?"

"He is so, and no wonder."

"Then they're wanting a man to carry out the execution of Macdonald and Reeves?" questioned Johnny.

Again they regarded his face, with the beautiful eyes and long, ragged hair.

"They are, but they'll wait many a long day, I'm thinking," said the bearded man. "There's few men would take up a job the like of that. Hanging Johnny, he was a murthering devil for you. They say he was killed by the brother of Tim Derrybawn, and if he was, it was what he deserved. Did you hear of that business, now?"

"I did not," said Johnny. His eyes were shining with excitement. "Where are Macdonald and Reeves under sentence of death?" he asked.

"They're at Mountjoy Prison—God help them," answered the man with the beard.

Johnny said nothing else. He picked up his bag and went out of the room.

The woman was coming down the stairs, a candle in her hand.

"The poor creature is better," she whispered. "Don't be waking her now and you going upstairs, for she's in a grand sound sleep."

"I'm glad," said Johnny hurriedly. "Is there a pen in the house I could borrow a loan of?"

The woman seemed a little disappointed at his lack of ardour over Anna.

"You to be thinking of pens and your wife scarcely alive upstairs!" she retorted. "But, bedad, there's pens to be had for the asking."

She led him into another room where there was a table littered with papen. A pen lay among them, with a twisted nib, and there was a broken-necked bottle of ink.

"That's all there is," said the woman; "we don't have much call here to be writing."

Johnny sat down and took from his bag a cardboard box.

He opened it and there was a pile of printed forms inside. He selected one and began to fill it in laboriously in a large, scrawling handwriting:

I also beg leave to state that my terms are as follows: £10 for the execution, and £5 if condemned is reprieved, together with all travelling expenses.
Awaiting your reply,
I am, sir,
Your obedient servant.

That was all printed. He had only to fill in the dates and the name of the prison. He signed his name "Johnny Cregan," and never thought of abbreviating it to "John."

"They know me," he murmured to himself. "They'll give me the job." He addressed the letter to the Sheriff of Dublin.

Before he resigned, before Tim Derrybawn had been killed, and a sudden distaste for his calling had grown on him, he had never had to apply for work. But he had kept the printed circulars he had used in his earlier days, and he considered it proper to employ one of them now.

He slept that night in a room next to Anna's. Once or twice he awoke and the feeling of loneliness was terrible. She had grown as much part of him as his arms and legs.

But he saw her in the morning, and his relief at her improvement was so great that he nearly shouted aloud.

She was sitting up in bed, dressed in a torn and dirty nightgown. Her face was very pale and her hair hung down her back in a matted tangle.

"Oh, Johnny," she said, "what has happened? Tell me all about it."

"You turned sick, darling. I was scared to death, so in two hop skips of a lame beggar I brought you here. And you're better, thanks be to God."

She frowned anxiously.

"But, Johnny, how are we going to pay for these rooms? I'm so worried about it. Do you think my best dress—?"

"Och, darling," he cried, "be easy now about that. They're doing all this for love of you, and why wouldn't they indeed?"

"It's very nice of them," she said, "but it's charity, you know." She moved her head restlessly on the pillow.

"What ails you, darling?" asked Johnny, tenderly anxious.

"Oh, this bed's so filthy I feel I can't lie comfortable in it. And my hair is in such a state. Do comb it out, Johnny, and plait it. My hands are so silly and weak!"

"I wouldn't be touching your hair, Anna. I love to see it hanging loose. It's like them pictures of mermaids I seen in a book."

"Oh, don't talk nonsense," she fretted; "it's collecting all the dirt."

Hastily he got her comb out of her brown paper parcel and tried clumsily to separate and braid the thick, springy hair.

"Make them give me clean blankets," she ordered. "These make me feel sick!"

"I will, darling. Let you be easy now, and don't be worrying your head over anything. Are you comfortable now?" He surveyed the loose, lumpy plait with pride.

"It's a bit better," she said. "Thank you, Johnny."

But her recovery was very slow. She had a robust constitution which threw off the effects of starvation and exhaustion bravely enough, but she could not keep her mind from the problem of money, and other petty worries. So, for many days she lay in bed, querulous and exacting, and bitterly critical of her surroundings.

She drove her rough nurse to the verge of exasperation by her anxiety for perfect cleanliness and her horror of dust.

"Look at the floor, Mrs. Mulvanney," she would say. "How can you just give it a wipe over like that, and leave half the dust still there, and half flying about in the air. It will settle on tables and things."

"Ah, be easy now," soothed the woman, "and don't be fashing yourself over them kinds of things."

"But you never sweep under the bed. I'm going to lean over and look. It must be in a filthy state."

She hung over the edge of the bed and peered as far as she could underneath it. Mrs. Mulvanney looked on, with a sort of pitying amusement.

"Come and look at this!" cried Anna. "It hasn't been touched for years. There's mounds of black dust, and old broken bottles and things. Really, Mrs. Mulvanney, a woman of your age should be ashamed to have things in such a disgusting state."

"Now you leave off talking that nonsense," Mrs. Mulvanney was stung to retort. "You should take shame to yourself to be talking that way to me, me that has put two husbands under the sod, and reared more childer than you could count on the fingers of your two hands, and you a bit of a girlee that's not borne your first child. Let you keep your mouth shut now about the things that are round you, or you'll find yourself in a hard place one fine day I'm thinking."

Anna grew a little pink.

"Well, will you please get a dustpan and sweep under the bed," she said more humbly. "I can't sleep over that dirt."

"You're after sleeping over it for the last week then, and no harm come to you," said Mrs. Mulvanney. She flounced indignantly out of the room.

"That dust was there in my mother's time, so it was," she muttered to herself, "and I've slept on the top of it for fifty-seven years. Herself and her dustpans!"

Every day Johnny spent hours by his wife's bedside. They would make plans for the future, and now, Anna was despondent and anxious and Johnny was the comforter.

One morning a letter came to him which he read with difficulty, but with great excitement. He did not show it to Anna.

"I wish I hadn't got ill," sighed Anna, when he came into her room. "I've never been ill before. And I'm stronger than you, Johnny, so I don't know why you didn't get poorly too."

"Och, I'm more used to it," he explained. "I tramped for weeks when I was a young lad."

"Do you know," she said anxiously; "I don't know anything about you, Johnny. Isn't it funny the way I married you without asking any questions? But I'd like to hear about it all, now."

"Ah, let it be, Anna. I'll tell you another time. Shall we talk about the way we'll be living in another year? Do you know, I've remembered something."

"What's that, Johnny?"

"Why, I used to be mending shoes a long time ago. I wouldn't say but I've not forgotten the way of it now. Maybe, we could buy a shop and set up a cobbler's trade."

"That would be nice, Johnny, but it's silly to talk, when we've got no money. Oh, I'm worried sick to think of that. I'm sure you won't be able to get work in Dublin, Johnny. I can't think how I was ever such a fool as to think of walking all the way on a chance."

"Anna," he said abruptly, "if I brought you a whole handful of bank-notes, would you be worrying your head over the way I got them?"

She flashed a suspicious glance at him.

"You wouldn't steal, Johnny."

"I'd do more than that for you," he said; "but suppose it was honestly that I got them?"

She laid her head back on the pillow and closed her eyes.

"How silly you talk, Johnny. Of course, if you earned some money, I'd go crazy mad with joy."

"Whatever way I earned it?" he insisted.

"Of course, I wouldn't mind how you earned it. But what's the use of talking? You could never do it."

He left her that day with a light heart.

Time passed, and Anna still lay feeble and tortured by anxiety. One day Johnny accosted Mrs. Mulvanney on the stairs.

"I'm going away this afternoon," he said. "Look after Anna while I'm away. I'll be back some time to-morrow."

Mrs. Mulvanney had no high opinion of men, and looked on Johnny as a particularly untrustworthy specimen of his sex.

"What are you going for?" she questioned sharply.

"Business," said Johnny, "very important business that I wouldn't like to be talking about."

"Well," said the woman suspiciously, "mind you do come back."

Johnny flushed angrily, and she continued: "I don't trust you, so I don't. I don't like the loony ways of you, nor the green eyes of you, nor the bag you do be carrying about with you. That's the truth for you, now."

Johnny turned away, not deigning to argue with her.

"If you don't come back to-morrow," she called shrilly after him, "I'll set the police on you. I've seen too many young girls—"

Anna was surprised and a little annoyed when she heard of Johnny's departure.

"He might have told me," she said. "I wonder why he went. I expect he was tired of hanging round here doing nothing, though he generally likes that better than anything else. I hope he'll take care of himself."

Mrs. Mulvanney saw, with a certain disappointment, that a single doubt never entered her head.

The next afternoon Johnny came back. Mrs. Mulvanney tried to waylay him on the stairs, but he raced past her. His eyes were wild with excitement, and Mrs. Mulvanney was so interested that she followed him to Anna's door and put her ear to the keyhole.

Anna was sitting up in bed knitting a grey sock, for even in her illness she could not bear to be idle.

"Where have you been, Johnny?" she asked. "Why didn't you tell me you were going away?"

Johnny dropped on his knees beside the bed and flung his arms round her.

"Oh, I was lonely without you, Anna."

"But what have you been doing? Tell me quick."

"Shut your eyes then, darling, and when I say 'Open,' you'll find a surprise."

"Oh, I can't waste time in this foolery," she said irritably. "Show me what you've got sensibly, if you can."

"I will not. You must shut your eyes."

Unwillingly she obeyed.

"You're no better than a child, Johnny," she murmured.

He took something from his pocket and laid it on her pillow.

"Open!" he commanded triumphantly.

She unclosed her eyes, and her fingers flew to the thing he had placed on the pillow.

"Johnny, it's notes! It's money! What have you done?"

Her eyes grew almost fearful.

"I'm after earning some money, Anna. I'll tell you all about it. You needn't worry. Aren't you glad?"

"Glad?" She fingered the crisp notes, counting them over and over again. "Johnny, it's just the saving of us. Now, tell me how you did it, quick. I can't wait till I hear."

"Well, Anna," he said slowly. "It's hard to tell you. I don't know how you'll take it, darling."

"Oh, Johnny, you haven't—"

"No, it's not that. It's honest work, Anna. I—I executed the two convicts, Macdonald and Reeves, at Mountjoy Prison, this morning at eight o'clock."

He paused, and she gaped at him with puzzled eyes.

"You hung them, Johnny?"

"Hanged," he corrected gently. "Yes, Anna. You see, before I ever met you—you won't be angry?—I was executioner. Then I resigned, but when you got ill I was crazy to earn something for you, the way it would ease your mind; so when I heard the other executioner Moore had resigned, I wrote to the Sheriff of Dublin, and he give me the post again by reason of me being well known without a stain on my character. So that was how I got the money. But, darling, if so be you don't like it, I'll not hang another man ever again. I'll burn the ropes and straps I have in my bag."

"But, I remember now father used to talk about the other executioner before Moore," said Anna non-committally. "Cregan, his name was."

"Cregan's my name, Anna. But I changed it for you the way you wouldn't be set against me. Everyone in this country would like to see me dead, so they would."

"Oh!" she said.

"Do you mind it?" he insisted eagerly. "Are you angry with me, Anna girl? I'll resign straight away—"

"No," she said slowly. "I don't mind. The post of executioner is a Government one, so it's quite respectable. I don't hold with people who speak about a hangman as if he was a murderer out of jail."

He seized her again in his arms, and kissed her white face and her hair.

"When you get well," he whispered, "we can go to Dublin and set up the cobbler's shop."

Chapter XII

A week later, Johnny went into Dublin to see about the shop. Anna insisted on accompanying him, and was with difficulty prevailed on to stay behind.

"You're not fit for a long day in the town," argued Mrs. Mulvanney. "Better let your husband see to it."

"I know he'll make a mess of it," said Anna. "Johnny, don't do anything silly. Make as good a bargain as possible, and don't spend any of the money until you have to. Oh, I wish I could do it myself."

Johnny knew Dublin fairly well. He made unerringly for the back streets, the slums where all the refuse of the city is thrown together in a vile, hideous mass.

He walked thoughtfully through narrow lanes and gutters until he came to St. Brigid Street, the darkest, dirtiest of them all. On either side of him tall, narrow tenement houses rose up, till you could see only a small oblong of sky between them. Bits of refuse of the city, naked and dirty, stared curiously after him as he went along, and then returned to their occupation of fishing in the gutter. He glanced quite casually at them. They were his own people, and he felt at home amongst them. The smell of filth and decay was the atmosphere he had been reared in, so he took no heed of it.

In the middle of the houses on the left-hand side was one much smaller than the others. He went closer to it and saw that it was a dingy shop, with just one floor above it. The door was so low that he had to bend his head to go in. Inside, it was dirty, unaccountably dark, and again so low that his head banged against the ceiling when he stood upright.

An old man shuffled forward to attend to him, peering at him through the gloom.

Johnny had to listen to a long string of lamentations and railings against fate and the police.

The old man did not mind telling Johnny that he had been a seller of unlicensed tobacco. He had lost a great deal of money over the business. He believed that the police—bad cess to them—had their eyes on him. He wanted to leave the shop hut where in the name of the Saints would he go, and he with not five shillings in the pockets of him?

Then Johnny spoke, and the old man listened with great satisfaction. He would be delighted to sell the whole concern to Johnny for five guineas.

"I'll throw in the wee bit of furniture I have upstairs," he conceded.

Johnny thanked him profusely.

It did not occur to him to examine the top floor. "And listen now," the old man whispered hoarsely, clutching Johnny's arm, "there's a wee store of tobacco I have in under the counter there. I'll give that to you along with the shop, if so be you'll let me take a wee scrap of it in my pockets. It'll be great company for me, so it will, and I walking the roads."

"Where will you be going when you leave this?" asked Johnny in the low voice that the musty darkness seemed to demand.

"Sorra a know I knows. But it's glad I'll be to get out of this place. It's a sad place. There's no luck in it."

As Johnny stepped into the street, he turned back and saw the old man stooping in the doorway, brown and withered, blinking at the light.

The thought came to Johnny that perhaps the shop had made him like that, bent and decayed, and perhaps the gloom and the dust would creep into his blood also.

Anna had quite recovered when he brought her to Dublin and guided her to St. Brigid Street.

"It's only a wee bit of a place, darling," he told her, "but it will do fine for us and we'll have a trade going in three swishes of a cow's tail."

At first she answered hopefully, but as the streets grew dirtier and darker, she bit her lips and frowned.

"Here we are," said Johnny as they turned the corner into St. Brigid Street.

"Oh, Johnny," she said.

"What is it, agra?"

"Those children! Look at them. They've got hardly any clothes on."

He looked at the fighting, bony creatures with new interest.

"That's true, Anna. Sure the people—God help them—haven't money enough to put the clothes on them."

"But that's terrible!" she said. "Why don't they work?"

"Is it work?" he repeated in astonishment.

"Johnny, how can they watch their children grow up so wretched and wicked? It's just idle, good-for-nothing people they are here."

Vaguely troubled by her distaste, he put his arm round her. "Let you not be minding them, Anna. Here's the shop, now, and I've the key of it with me."

"Let's get inside quickly then, for the smell in this street is terrible," said Anna.

"Smell? Och, you'll get used to it."

She looked rather angry, and turned impatiently to the shop. The shop door was the only entrance to the house, and to reach the upper rooms, you had to go right through the shop and up a twisted flight of stairs.

A little knot of women had gathered on the opposite side of the street to stare at the newcomers.

From the windows of the tenement houses, faces protruded, hungry, unkempt and rather hostile.

Anna hastily shut the door of the shop and stood in the darkness with Johnny.

"Here's where I'll be working," explained Johnny. "We can buy some tools, and I'll start as soon as you like."

"We shall have to clean it up first," she said briskly. "It's thick with dust and dirt. I'm going upstairs. Didn't the old man leave his furniture there?"

"He did," Johnny admitted, rather conscience stricken.

They climbed the broken stairs and came to a door at the top. Anna pushed it open, and they entered a room with a window at one end, and another door beside the fireplace. A table stood in the centre, one of its legs supported by a brick. The remains of a meal was set out on it, and smuts dotted the chipped white plates. The fireplace was full of ashes, and dust lay thick over everything.

Two chairs, one of them minus its front legs, completed the furnishing.

"How disgusting!" said Anna. "We must start on the place to-morrow, Johnny, and clean it all thoroughly. I don't suppose it's been swept for years. Ugh!" They opened the other door, and found a smaller room, with nothing in it except a bed. The blankets on it were almost black, and it lay just as the old man had tumbled out of it on the morning of his departure.

"He seemed in a great hurry to be gone," Anna remarked, looking at this.

"So he would be, too. I wouldn't care to be working below in this shop and no one up here."

"What are you talking about, Johnny?"

His eyes became dark and unfathomable. The troubled forehead and the mouth expressed foreboding and a vague fear.

"There's things—" he muttered, "the old man said there's no luck in this place."

She was not listening to him.

"It's not so bad, Johnny," she said. "We'll make it do. And I'll tell you what we'll do. We won't move, even when we're getting more money. We'll save it all, and perhaps when we can afford it, we'll get a better house and keep more style." She laughed as she said this, but Johnny did not respond to her mood.

His face was still troubled and a little unhappy.

"Anna," he said, "I don't want the neighbours to know who I am. Will you keep up being Mrs. Croghan, and they needn't know they're living foreninst Johnny Cregan, the Hangman? Will you do this for me, Anna?"

"Very well, if you feel like that about it. I suppose it would be hard if they knew. They would start rows, which would be very annoying. But Johnny"—her voice took on a firmer tone—"when you say 'neighbours' I suppose you mean those horrible creatures that stared at us when we came in. I tell you once and for all that I wouldn't have any truck with the like of them if I was paid for it. Dirty, good-for-nothing idlers, that's what they are. I wouldn't have them inside my doors. I'm sure they're dishonest and bad too. We'll keep ourselves to ourselves, Johnny, while we're here."

"Och, now," he reasoned, recognising another complication. "We can't live here without any friends, Anna. They're good people enough, so they are. You'd like some women to be gossiping with, and they running in and out of the house. You wouldn't care to be lonesome while I'm below in the shop?"

She turned indignantly on him.

"What way are you talking, Johnny? Is it make friends with those women who haven't a bit of shame or honesty to them? I'm not proud, but I couldn't do that. Can't you understand, Johnny? I don't know how you can talk so."

"Don't be angry with me, Anna," he came and stood beside her, putting his arm round her waist.

The action was almost timid, as if he feared a rebuff. Here in this squalid room, she seemed so much further away from him than in the garden off Murphy's grocery store, or even in Mrs. Mulvanney's pub. Those days seemed quite, far off, now, as if they had happened a few years ago.

A baby was wailing in the next house. They could hear the mother's weary scolding and a screech as she slapped it.

In spite of her condition, Anna insisted on tackling the rough work that lay before them in the house. Johnny, all tender anxiety for her, tried honestly to save her the heaviest labour, but his slipshod, inefficient methods irritated her beyond endurance. And at last all the dust and rubbish and accumulated filth was cleared out, and Anna was almost satisfied. She bought new crockeryware out of the remaining five guineas, and a set of tools for Johnny. She also invested in a large dresser and a wash-tub. Then she made Johnny clean the shop window, so that a little light filtered into the dusky interior.

In the evenings she knitted tiny garments and Johnny would sit at the other side of the fire, dreaming silently, his hands hanging relaxed between his knees.

Sometimes they talked about the child.

"We'll call him James, after father," Anna decided. She knew it was a custom to call children after their grandfathers, and she always liked to do customary things.

"If it's a girl," said Johnny, "it will be called Anna or nothing."

"Come to that," she said, "what about John? We might alter it to Jack, so as to be a bit different from you."

"Or Michael," he suggested wistfully. "Anna, do let it be Michael. It's a fine name. I've always thought I'd like one of my childer to be called Michael."

He was very excited about the coming event. The child would mean a great deal to him. Anna never guessed at the dreams and plans that formed in his head as he sat in the shop.

He showed her at this time a very fine delicacy and consideration that surprised her.

One evening they had been talking about the child, and gradually their voices had dropped into silence. Anna was interested in the wee flannel petticoat she was making.

Johnny looked up at her suddenly.

"Anna," he said, "will you do something?"

"What is it?"

He took something very slowly out of his pocket. "Will you wear this round you, Anna, next to your skin?"

She looked up and saw that he was holding an old charred piece of rope.

"What's that dirty thing, Johnny?"

He caressed it with his long, sensitive fingers.

"This rope has hanged twenty men," he said. "I've used it myself in eleven executions. It got burnt at the execution of Shawn Farrell when they set the scaffold house on fire." His thoughts had drifted away again. He stared broodingly into space, running his fingers up and down the rope.

"How horrible!" she said energetically. "I don't like you going round with it in your pocket, Johnny. Throw it into the fire."

"You don't understand," he said in horror. "This rope has great luck in it. I wouldn't move three steps without it, so I wouldn't. And Anna, it will bring great good if you'll be wearing it next your skin, and you going about the house. Them that wear the rope at your time"—his voice grew lower—"never have a dead baby born to them."

"I wish you wouldn't talk such nonsense," she said, colouring. "It's not reverent, and I'm sure you oughtn't. Do throw it into the fire, Johnny, and have done with it. It's a horrible thing."

She reached forward to take it from him, but with a quick, defensive movement, he snatched it away and put it back in his pocket. He did not speak of it again.

Anna bore her pregnancy remarkably well. She looked healthy and indulged in no morbid doubts or fears. Johnny called in an old woman to attend to her when the time drew near, and waited in the shop restless and wildly excited. He was not really anxious, for he did not believe that Anna would fail. She was very strong.

And all went well. When he was allowed to see her, he approached the room on tiptoe as if it were the shrine of something very beautiful and holy.

Anna was lying back on her pillows. Her hair hung round her like a cloud, and the baby lay in the crook of her arm, its head covered with fine red down.

Johnny stopped short in awed admiration and worship, scarcely daring to approach. "It's a boy," she said, smiling at him, rather wearily, but indomitably.

"Oh," breathed Johnny, "you look like the Holy Virgin in the pictures."

"You oughtn't to speak like that," she said faintly.

Very gently, trying to subdue his passion, he knelt down by the bed and put his forehead down on her firm hand.

"This is wonderful," he whispered. "I know that now we're going to be very happy."

Chapter XIII

"Good morning, Mrs. Croghan," said Mrs. Carey.

She paused in the doorway, for she was taking a certain amount of risk in calling on Mrs. Croghan on Monday morning.

"It's a fine morning," she went on. "Why wouldn't you be out, now, enjoying it with the rest of us?"

Anna, bending over the wash-tub, her arms immersed in soapy, darkening water, did not reply.

"Ah, well," said Mrs. Carey, "maybe you're right. And is that the child? Isn't it fine and strong he's growing, and taking after his father. The fine man he is, Mrs. Croghan."

Anna squeezed and pounded Johnny's shirt with a brisk efficiency that discouraged conversation.

Michael, aged five and a half years, shouted delightedly.

"Sure, you make me feel ashamed, Mrs. Croghan," said Mrs. Carey admiringly, "you beating the dirt out of that shirt as if Johnny was going to wear it to court to-morrow and it cleaned and starched."

"There's no reason to feel ashamed, when you could be doing the like this moment," said Anna briefly.

"So I could now," agreed Mrs. Carey in a surprised tone.

But she smiled—in the same pitying, amused way that Mrs. Mulvanney had smiled when Anna scolded her for the dirt under the bed.

"Amn't I the lazy woman to be coming in and wasting your time, when I've work beyond there that would surprise you, the way it never gets done," she remarked. "But, sure, Danny doesn't care if the dinner's not cooked and he coming home. He's not like some men that do be grumbling over this thing and that thing, the way there's no pleasing them if the Saint Brigid herself was to be cooking the dinner for them."

She glanced sharply at Anna's bent back that seemed to radiate energy and perseverance. "I'm thinking now that Johnny's an easy one to please?" she hinted.

"He's the same as other men," said Anna, brusquely. She wrung out Johnny's shirt and placed it with other rinsed garments on a white enamelled tray.

"Now I'll tell you a queer thing," began Mrs. Carey. "I had it from my father and he lived in the town where it happened. There was a woman in Clommel—"

"Michael," said Anna sharply, "will you take that bit of coke out of your mouth this minute. Go and sit on that chair now and don't be bold or I'll slap you."

Offended at the snub, Mrs. Carey moved to the door.

"I beg your pardon, Mrs. Croghan," she said stiffly, "for taking up of your time. Another day, when you wouldn't be working so hard, maybe I'll drop in and tell you the story. It's a grand story. Maybe Johnny would like to hear it as well. Good day to you, Mrs. Croghan."

She went down the stairs and through the shop. Johnny started working in a great hurry as she came in, and stopped directly he saw who she was.

Mrs. Carey stepped across the street and into one of the houses on the opposite side. She climbed to the top floor and opened a door in the passage.

Here three women were gathered round a meagre fire. One of them was very feeble and old, and lay back in her chair, her hands folded on her lap.

"Won't you have a drop of tea, Mrs. Carey?" she invited as the newcomer entered the room.

"Is it drinking tea you are at this hour of the morning, Mrs. Rooney?"

"And why wouldn't I be drinking tea? I'm after eating nothing all the morning. When there's not a man about the house, it's queer the ways you do be getting into. I get out of my bed that late these days, me that would be rising with the daylight when Peter—God rest him—was alive and he going to his work early in the morning."

"Them were the grand days for you, Mrs. Rooney," sympathised one of the younger women. "I wouldn't wonder but you were a mighty fine woman in those times."

The old woman nodded, well pleased, and leaned back in the shadows. The room was large, and the small, dirty windows let in only a thin ray of light.

"I'm after spending an hour with Mrs. Croghan," began Mrs. Carey importantly.

"Is it going in on Mrs. Croghan and it Monday morning? Glory be, if she had the life of you, there'd be no wonder in it at all."

"There would not indeed. Mrs. Croghan's a mighty queer woman."

"Every Monday morning as ever is," said Mrs. Carey, as if telling something incredible, "she takes the clothes of herself and Johnny and the child and washes them in the tub. Now, will you tell me what's the good washing a man's trousers when it's as dirty or worse they'll be the next day?"

"And a man wouldn't deserve it," said Mrs. Finnigan.

"Working your fingers to the bone for them creatures! It's little they'd thank you for it."

"Though I wouldn't say but Johnny Croghan's a decent man, though maybe not quite right in his head," said Mrs. Donovan thoughtfully. She was the youngest of the three.

"Och, it's queer the way he does be going on," said Mrs. Carey; "sitting doing nothing he'll be for hours, staring with the big eyes of him as if he saw nothing. It would frighten you, so it would. But the woman he has there would be enough to drive a man crazy. Fussing over this thing and that thing she is from morning till night. Sure, what does it matter if the floor's clean or if it's not clean? Precious few men ever notice them kind of things."

"There'd be no wonder if she had him driven mad the way she does be going on," broke in Mrs. Donovan eagerly. "I'm wondering often what made him take up with her. It's a great pity he ever did, poor man, and he with a face on him that would take the heart out of your bosom. Often I'm sorry for him, for he's a decent man and a good man. He is so."

"Well, have you noticed the way he does be going off from here now and again," said Mrs. Carey mysteriously. "Staying away sometimes for four days together, he'll be. There's something odd in that."

"But it's little she seems to care about the way he does be going off," began Mrs. Donovan. The other women cast annoyed looks at her for trying to mitigate the mystery, so she added hastily: "but sure it's no wonder if he wants sometimes to get away from herself, and her dustpans and her wash-tubs. I'm thinking he must be glad to put a few miles of ground between himself and the sharp tongue of her."

"Do you remember when she first came to this street and took over old George Kennedy's shop?" reflected Mrs. Finnigan. "Mighty proud and stiff she was in those days. She wouldn't have the likes of us inside her doors at all. Herself that's no better than the rest of us. If she sets herself up to be more of a lady than myself or yourself, Mrs. Carey, why doesn't she take herself off to Merrion Square or to a shop in Grafton Street. Will you tell me that?"

"Always a scolding look in her eye she had for us. I wouldn't scrub this floor if it were a hundred pounds she'd give me for it, I wouldn't, so. Herself and her clean floors!"

"Whisht, now!" said Mrs. Donovan, "there's Johnny Croghan in the door of the shop. Tired he looks, God help him."

There was a universal rush to the window.

Johnny stood just outside his own doorway. His shoulders were hunched from much stooping, and he stood blinking in the bright air after the darkness, just as the old man Kennedy had done. That evening, Anna sat by the fire, darning as usual. The red light flickered over the room, half revealing its clean bareness. It was growing very dim, because she never lit the candles before it was too dark to see at all. She was alone, for Michael was playing outside and Johnny was down in the shop.

A wooden work-box stood beside her, which she kept in scrupulous order. As she searched in it for some grey wool she saw an envelope lying in the bottom. She hesitated, then, smiling a little, she picked it up and drew out the letter it contained. It was old and limp, and she knew by heart the words which were written on it in a firm, untutored hand:

BALLYBOULTEEN,
JULY, 1873.

Anna Girl,

I'm hoping God will guide this letter to you wherever you are. Jamesy Lee is leaving this place and going to Dublin, so I am sending this with him to give to you if so be he should find you.

Well, Anna girl, I'm sorry I let my temper run away with me that day when you told me, but I was in a fine rage—God forgive me—for I'd always hoped you'd do better than that, and Mat Cave fretting his heart about you, the poor boy.

But that's over and done with, and I'd be pleased to let bygones be bygones.

It's lonesome now in the evenings, now that yourself and your mother are gone. The neighbours are very kind, but it's not the same.

Will you come back to me, Anna, and take over the shop like you were going to?

I'm getting older and I don't seem able to run the business like I used to, and it's glad and proud I'll be to see you at the head of it, like we used to talk about. That wretched fellow who took you away from me will have made you unhappy by now or my name's not James Murphy. He hadn't the look of a decent man in the face of him. I never want to set eyes on him again, so leave him, and you needn't be too proud to come back to your old father, for you would not find the door shut on you. I've been a long time writing this and thinking how to spell the words and divil a line more can I write, so no more from

        Your loving father,

           James Murphy.

Two years ago, Jamesy Lee, ragged and looking for work, had found his way into St. Brigid Street, and had seen the name "Croghan" painted over the dingy, poky little shop. Anna had never shown the letter to Johnny, and she had never answered it. She had not the kind of eyes that can read between the written words. Johnny's step sounded on the stairs and she put the letter back in the box.

He came in and went to the fire with a little shiver.

"Johnny," she said reprovingly, "you're up half an hour early."

"I'm after closing up early," he said. "Sure, I knew nobody would be coming, and it's mighty cold down there."

"Oh, Johnny," she said irritably, "that's such bad business. You never seem to care anything about the shop, and it's our living, you know. Your other work doesn't bring us so very much, and what it does bring I'm saving in a drawer yonder in the dresser."

"Ah, well," he said. He sat down by the fire and stared into it, his hands hanging between his knees. The attitude was one that particularly annoyed her. Presently he glanced up at her energetic fingers.

"Are you very busy, Anna?" he asked, almost wistfully. She laid by the finished sock and took up another.

"You're always at something," he went on. "Don't you ever feel you'd like to rest like the other women round? You wouldn't see them doing half the work you do."

"Do you mean Mrs. Carey, and Mrs. Donovan, and that lot?" she burst out. "The shiftless, lazy crowd, that's what they are! They have nice homes, haven't they! I've been in some of them and they nigh made me ill."

"Yet they're happy enough, it seems," said Johnny.

"Happy! With dust and dirt fit to choke you in every corner of the house, and the floors littered with rubbish that the children bring in with them off the roads. You talk so silly, Johnny, sometimes. I'm sorry for the men that have to go back to those places at night. I'll be bound there's never a decent cooked meal for them. They care about nothing, those women, except to be running about colloguing and gossiping with each other the whole day, with never a thought for their husbands or their children. It's a disgrace to see them. You come into a clean, decent room after your work, with not a speck of dirt anywhere. I wonder what way you'd be talking if I set a few cold potatoes in front of you for supper and nothing else. That's what you'd have to put up with if I spent my days running round after Mrs. Carey and the like of her, instead of doing my work and my duty, and keeping things nice for you."

The long tirade surprised him, for Anna was a woman of few words.

"I know that well," he said loyally. "It's a lucky man I am to have a wife the like of you, and such a grand home. Only I thought you might be tired. I came up early because I thought to myself we'd have a quiet time together, talking maybe. We don't seem to have the talks now we did be holding in the old days, Anna."

She broke off a strand of wool with her teeth.

"I haven't the time to talk," she said, "and it's a lucky thing for you that I haven't. Where would you be if there was no one to darn your socks for you? I like you to look decent and respectable, and I'm proud of you among the men round here with the coat on their backs all in holes, and the flesh of their bodies showing through in the bitter weather. It's little enough their wives care for that."

Johnny turned his eyes to the fire again. The familiar brooding, dreamy look came over his face. It was the beautiful face now of a poet.

"I wish he would do something," Anna thought vexedly. "I must get something for him to do in the evenings. I can't bear to see him sitting there, staring at the fire, like no sane man does. He mustn't close early another night."

Johnny looked up and saw her eyes fixed on him. His face awoke instantly to life and the troubled restlessness it often wore.

"Anna, darling," he said yearningly, "put down that work and come on to my knee for a few minutes before the child will be home on us. There's things I feel I could say to you with my arms round you, and it's precious little time I have like that with you these days."

"Arrah, Johnny, leave me alone now. You know I haven't the time to waste. I have the supper to get. Glory be, it's past six and it not on the pan."

"I'd rather be without the supper," said Johnny.

He got up and bent over her. In a moment his arms would have been round her neck.

"Will you stand out of my light, Johnny?" she said.

He drew away, and stood looking at her with the eyes of an animal that cannot understand.

"Anna," he said in a very low voice, "you've changed since we were married. You love me still, don't you? You'd always love me?"

When he said anything particularly silly, it was Anna's custom not to answer him. She did not believe in wasting words.

"I bought some sausages for your supper," she said brightly. "I know you like them."

Johnny did not answer. To her surprise, he gave a little sigh and walked out of the room.

Anna took her father's letter out of the workbox. She read it through once more, then she tore it in half and dropped it into the fire. She would never tell Johnny how much she had given up for him, because she loved him better than anything else in the world.

And men never guess at these things.

Chapter XIV

"Johnny," said Anna at lunch next day, "I've been thinking over what we said about the neighbours yesterday, how dirty and ignorant they are, and I'm going to have Mrs. Carey and Mrs. Donovan and Mrs. Doyle to drink a cup of tea with me this afternoon."

He looked pleased and surprised.

"Maybe, now, you're getting more sociable," he said. "I'd be glad if you'd make friends with some of the women, Anna. They'd be company for you."

"They would not then. It's not that I'm having them for. But I've been looking at the children, Johnny, and it's shameful the way they go about in rags. Little heathens they are. So, I'm going to teach the women how to make clothes. It's disgraceful for them to be bringing children into the world, and then not caring if they die of cold because they're too lazy to make as much as a woollen petticoat."

Johnny stared, too amazed to speak.

"Later on," continued Anna, full of her new idea, "maybe I'll teach them how to cook and keep their rooms clean. I can't live any longer here, without trying to make them ashamed of their slack ways."

Johnny blinked in a puzzled way.

"You're a good woman, Anna," he said slowly.

"I try to do my duty, I hope."

Johnny sat with his elbow on the table, resting his chin on his hand, and gazing down at the floor.

Anna bustled about, taking the dishes from the table. "It's time for you to be in the shop," she said presently. "You'd best be going, Johnny, for I see Mrs. Doyle coming down the street, and I don't want you to be here."

He heaved himself up and walked slowly to the door; his body never would hold itself upright. The shoulders were stooped, and the large limbs seemed to hang and drag loosely.

At the door, he turned.

"Anna, you'll not mention the hangman—ever? Sometimes I'm feared to death you'll let it slip out of your mouth, and you colloguing with Mrs. Carey over the cups."

"Johnny!" she said, hurt and offended.

"Och, I know you wouldn't," he apologised hastily. "You see, we would have to leave this place if it was known."

"Come, Johnny, don't be silly. There's no need to feel like that about an honest job. After all," with a slight pride, "it's Government work."

"They'd be casting it up at the child," he muttered. "'Hanging Johnny' was the name they put on me in the old days. Oh, they hated me." Resentment and a hurting memory of that mortification and ridicule burned in his eyes. "Now everyone knows 'Hanging Johnny' is back at his work, but no one outside you knows that it's in this shop he's living."

His voice had sunk to a whisper.

"You're so queer sometimes," said Anna. "Often I think you ought to give up the hanging job, you get so funny about it. Only it would be a pity to lose the money."

"It would so," he agreed in his normal voice. "Och, I'm not

thinking of resigning yet awhile."

"I know the neighbours are wondering why you have to go away so often," she observed. "I'll have to think of a reason for when they ask me, though it's a hard thing to tell a lie. Now I hear someone at the shop door, and you're late already. I wish you'd take a bit more interest in the shop, Johnny. You know it's everything to us."

He opened the door, and she heard his slow footsteps on the stairs going down to the shop.

Anna bustled about the room, making up the fire and preparing knitting and sewing for the women. Michael sat in a corner playing with some bricks his father had planed for him, and crooning gently to himself.

Mrs. Doyle was the first to arrive. She waited at the shop door for Mrs. Carey and Mrs. Donovan and the three women came in together.

Anna found it difficult to start the proceedings.

There was a disposition to admire the room and criticise Michael. But at last, she helped them to put up some knitting, gave them a few instructions and took her own work out of her basket.

The women struggled with their stitches until her head was bent over the patch she was inserting in Michael's trousers. Then they leaned back in their chairs, enjoying the unwonted comfort. Their needles remained idle except when they were waved or pointed to emphasise a remark. Three times Anna steered the conversation off politics, knowing what that would lead to.

So it turned naturally to the topic of secondary importance—husbands.

"Danny, he came home last night in a tearing rage—" began Mrs. Carey.

"I know that indeed," said Mrs. Donovan, who lived on the

floor below, "for I heard him hollering to knock the house down, and the children scared out of their wits for fear he'd come down. Sam says, 'Danny has the drink taken surely,' he says—"

"He had not then," flared Mrs. Carey, "and it's a great shame and disgrace for you to be saying that, Honor Donovan. Is it drink? Now, doesn't the whole town know how Sam Donovan does be spending the evenings at Fogarty's pub. And if he goes in sober—it's not sober he comes out."

"Will you hold your tongue, Kitty Carey, and you the wife of the worst gambler in this town and maybe in Ireland itself? Taking the money you have in the old teapot under the bed he'll be, the way he'll have something to lose to Neil Fogarty. Taking the children's clothes to the pawnshop he'll be. Sure and doesn't the whole town know that?"

"May the devil blow the breeches off you, Honor Donovan, if so be you wear the like, for the things you're saying and the lies you're telling. Let you wait till I get at you. I've a fine sharp needle in my hand, and I'll stick it into the prying eyes of you." She got up and made a lunge at her insulter. Anna caught her by the arm.

"Sit down at once, Mrs. Carey, and don't behave like a child of two years old. It's a wonder you're not ashamed of yourself. Look at the way you have your wool tangled."

Mrs. Carey got to her feet, her face scarlet and angry. She could have understood an outburst of fury from Anna, either verbal or physical, but the calm, scathing tone roused a queer pride in her.

"I won't stay in this room another minute to be called names by you, Mrs. Croghan," she said. "You, an impudent little rapscallion setting up to be the better than the rest of us. You can take your knitting back. I wouldn't take it from you if you handed it to me made into the breeches. Good day to you, Mrs. Croghan."

She marched out of the room, leaving a slight tension behind her. Anna stitched on, her cheeks burning a little, and the women rather enjoyed her discomfiture.

"Well, now," said Mrs. Doyle, after a short silence. "Pat is a good husband to me, after all. We're as fond of each other as two cushat doves. In the evenings when I have the childer asleep, he'll be taking me on his knee, and the foolish things we do be saying to each other! Faith, it's as if we were young again and he courting me at my mother's house in Galway."

"Ah, there's things you can't be saying aloud," said Mrs. Donovan, "and a kiss will tell all you want and no harm done. Will you tell me how else a man is to know you're fond of him? It's precious little words count with him."

"Och, men are the great fools for all they do be talking of what they can do," said Mrs. Doyle. "But sure what's the good of grumbling, when the Lord made them that way, and won't be making them any different, I'm thinking, if we grumble till the world ends!"

Anna's needles clicked like a sane and healthy protest against this foolish sentimentality. The talk bored and annoyed her.

"Come now, Mrs. Croghan," said Mrs. Doyle, suddenly moved to appeal to her, "what do you think of it all?"

"I'm surprised at you both," Anna said tartly, "wasting your time talking nonsense. That's what you're doing all day, when your children haven't a rag to put on their backs. It's a disgrace to you to bring them up in the dirty, feckless homes you have here. Look at you now with those petticoats not begun. You should be ashamed when you look round at this room and at the child there dressed decently and warmly."

She had spoken sharply, but she had no idea of the effect it would produce.

The two women gave something like a howl of rage, and leaped to their feet.

"The Saints be my witness I won't stand here and be told by that one how to be rearing my childer, and what to be saying to the neighbours. Herself and her knitting!" blazed Mrs. Doyle.

"'Our children haven't a rag on their backs!' It's a wonder she dares to say a bold-faced thing the like of that. Come on out of this, Mrs. Doyle. Good day, Mrs. Croghan." They made for the door, their bare feet leaving a trail of muddy imprints.

Anna stood up and pushed the hair back from her forehead. She was feeling a little discouraged and disappointed because her grand project had failed. It would be hard to face Johnny and admit her defeat. But she heard him coming up from the shop, and she turned resolutely to meet him. She was never one to turn her back on difficulties.

"Why are you up so early?" she rapped out as he opened the door. A little puzzled by the sharpness of her tone, he answered that he had come upstairs for his awl. He had seen Mrs. Carey flounce angrily out of the house, followed presently by the other two women, but an instinctive delicacy, which might almost be called tact, kept him from asking any questions.

But Anna knew that he guessed what had happened and his silence irritated her.

"I really can't understand these people," she began, greasing the frying pan with some lard on paper. "They just walked out of the house, leaving their knitting, for no reason I can see. They were so rude, too."

"For no reason?" Johnny repeated. He could guess well enough what had occurred. He knew the hostility that Anna had inspired in all the neighbours, and he understood it, though he always defended her loyally when they tried to make him agree with them.

"They got angry, I suppose, over something I said, I can't remember what it was now. And, Johnny, they're so unreasonable. Do you know, last week Mrs. Heeney wouldn't let me look at her baby, when it had something wrong with it. I knew it had, because I heard it crying the whole of one day as if something hurt it. It died yesterday, poor little thing. These women don't take benefits when they can get them; it's so silly."

Bored by the conversation, Michael left his bricks and ran down into the street.

"Anna, when Mrs. Dillon had a baby didn't you go to her and say you wondered she dared bring a child into the world, when she couldn't hope to rear it, and wasn't six children enough for her?"

Johnny felt a queer, instinctive desire to justify the people he knew and understood.

"Yes, I did," she admitted. "Who told you?"

"Mrs. Dillon herself. They don't like having the like of that said to them, Anna."

"They can't have any feelings if they can deliberately kill their own children, which is what most of them seem to be doing. People ought not to have children if they aren't able to make them of some use in the world."

"Oh, Anna, I don't like to hear you talk so," he said, for her hard logic repelled him.

"But they're such fools, they won't listen to what I say," she went on, unheeding him. "After all, I've been to school and seen better things. I'd listen and profit, too, if I was in their places. But there, I really can't understand them at all."

"Well, you see, Anna," he tried awkwardly to explain, "they're proud, these women—"

"Proud! Talk sense, Johnny!"

But he was right. The people in St. Brigid Street were proud in their own way, and are to this day. Anna felt vaguely that his sympathy was not with her. She took the lump of bacon and began, rather fiercely, to cut off rashers.

Suddenly a shrill, savage sound floated up from the street. The sound of children quarrelling. Anna turned to the window.

"That's Michael's voice!" she said.

"Why wouldn't it be, now?"

"Why? Johnny, aren't you ashamed to see your son fighting with a mob of filthy little brats in the street?"

"There's no harm in it, Anna," he soothed. "When I was a wee lad, I used to be fighting with the neighbours' childer, the whole of the day, and sorra a word anyone ever said to me."

"Well, I won't have it." She leaned out of the window and called to the tangled, shouting group: "Michael, come in out of that this instant."

"Ah, leave him, Anna. Sure the child's only playing."

"The more shame to him. Be quiet, Johnny." She shook off his arm. "Come in at once, Michael. Do you hear me?"

A small figure detached itself from the struggling, uproarious mass and moved reluctantly to the shop, dragging its feet a little.

"Do you want them all tormenting the child about this?" pleaded Johnny, who recognised in the boy symptoms of his own sensitive dread of ridicule and mortification. "It's a coward they'll be calling him."

"He can stand it well enough. He's not silly enough to mind what these ragamuffins say."

"You're too hard with him, Anna."

She swung round, her hands on her hips.

"He's my child, and I won't have him playing with the children of all the drunkards and gamblers in the town. You can't understand, Johnny, you can't understand."

"He's my child," said Johnny fiercely, "and I'll not stop him playing with the only friends he'll ever have."

"He's not going to stay here all his life. I'm going to make something of him. Have you no ambition for him, at all?"

"I have not. Nor ever had for myself, either."

She said angrily, "I know that. Otherwise—"

But she could not be deliberately cruel. Even in her irritation she felt that she was dealing with something much weaker than herself.

Michael came in, kicking his feet and inclined to be sullen. "Why did you call me in, mother? Dan Heeney, he'll think I'm feard of him."

He stamped his foot on the floor and suddenly burst out:

"I don't want to wear my boots, mother. Need I wear my boots?"

"What do you mean, Michael? Of course you must wear your boots. And in this cold weather of all times."

"Dan laughed at me about the boots. They all go barefoot," said the child in a low voice, and the tears came into his eyes. "I went for him then."

He turned away from her, conscious of a certain sympathy in his father's eyes and Johnny caressed his sturdy well-fed body with hungry fingers.

Anna whispered authoritatively: "Don't encourage him, Johnny. He must learn to know better."

There was the sound of steps in the shop, and Johnny rose mutinously to his feet and went to the door.

"I'm going with daddy," said the child less tearfully.

"No, you're not. I want to talk to you, Michael."

Johnny closed the door slowly behind him.

"Now, Michael," said Anna, "you mustn't fight with those boys ever again. If you do I'll punish you."

"Why not?" he said sullenly.

"Because they're not our class. They're very low, horrid creatures, and we don't want to be friends with them. You see, Michael, one day we'll leave this place and go somewhere else where we can make friends. Perhaps I'll teach you to keep a shop—a proper grocer's shop, maybe."

"Must I not play with Dan and the others then at all?' he questioned, only half convinced.

"Oh yes, you can play with them. I don't suppose I can stop you doing that. It's just I hate to see you fighting."

"Daddy doesn't mind," he said.

"Don't take any notice of daddy," said Anna sharply. "He doesn't think like we do. He's not our—well, he's different. And Michael," her voice grew more gentle, "just because daddy's—different, will you promise never to go anywhere with him or do anything he'll ask you till you've asked me if you may. Just say 'I must ask mother.'"

"I'll do that," he promised, growing bored with the discussion.

"You'll remember, won't you?"

"Surely," said the pink, unformed mouth.

So Anna picked up her patching again, sure in her narrow ignorance that she had done the best thing for them all.

Chapter XV

Anna had a quick, flaming temper that burnt itself out in a few minutes. It was not in her nature to brood over injuries and keep her anger hot with memory.

She had almost forgotten the quarrel over Michael by the next day, and as Johnny did not speak of it, it never occurred to her that he was turning it over and over in his mind. Johnny, indeed, became very silent and morose during the days that followed. In the evenings he sat for hours beside the fire, his white hands, covered with incongruous blisters and scratches, hanging loosely. Sometimes Anna looked up from her work and saw his eyes fixed on her with a puzzled, resentful expression. Not that she could have analysed the expression even if she had noticed it. She never wondered to herself what Johnny was thinking of when he gazed into space with those brooding, visionary eyes. It still irritated her but she had grown accustomed to it now as one of "Johnny's ways" and had learned that it was useless to scold him for it.

He never went out in the evenings and he hardly ever moved out of this position or spoke to her until he went to bed. Once, however, something roused him to anger and a sharp outburst that surprised her.

They were sitting in silence as usual, one on either side of the fire. Anna always had an armless chair like those in village halls, and Johnny a low stool.

Michael was playing with his bricks in the middle of the floor. He was a plump, black-haired child with eyes like his father's, and a face that gave promise of his father's beauty. Suddenly Johnny opened his lips and said quite conversationally, "Anna, I'm thinking the child is growing to be the image of his father."

Anna glanced at the small figure, and her heart swiftly contracted.

Michael sat amongst the ruins of the crazy structure he had been building. His legs were wide apart, and his hands hung listlessly between his knees. He was staring at the fire, his eyes full of baby thoughts and dreams, miles away from the bare, dimly-lit room.

The likeness to Johnny was so complete that it brought a pain to her heart.

She lifted the child, shook him a little, and deposited him again on the floor. "Baby play with bricks," she commanded. "When I've finished what I'm doing, I'll hear you say your letters."

Michael began, quite placidly, to rebuild his tower, humming tunelessly under his breath.

Johnny looked up.

"Ah, leave the child alone, will you?" he said almost angrily. "Will you always be after him, the way he'll never have the time to think over anything for himself?"

Anna was full of a new trouble. The likeness to Johnny which had shone out suddenly in Michael and disappeared was, to her, a danger-signal.

"We must make something of Michael," she said rather feverishly. "Maybe we could learn him to be a clerk—"

"Ah, be quiet, woman," he broke in roughly. "You and your

clerks! I know well enough what's in your mind. You don't want him to follow his father. You're afraid to see him grow like me—a failure in everything."

The choked passion in his voice slightly astonished her.

"What's the matter with you, Johnny—"

He stood up, breathing hard.

"Oh, I'm going out of this," he said. "There's no peace here."

He swung out of the room, and Anna frowned a little and threaded her needle.

She was wishing that Johnny had not gone out in the rain. He might catch cold, and he was not very strong.

"I'll make up a nice fire for him," she thought, "and put his other coat out to warm. He'll be wet through when he comes back with only those thin clothes on. He's like a child to be going off like that in a rage."

She had been too honest to deny to Johnny that she was alarmed at the symptoms of his dreamy laziness they had seen in Michael. But his words had no effect on her, because her love for him had never once faltered through the six years of their married life. It had only subtly changed, for it had become the love of a mother for a very dear child.

An hour later Johnny came back, morose, but quite normal. After that things went on as usual, except that he became, if possible, more silent, more shut into himself. He grew lax and disinterested in his work. Often Anna would go down to the shop and find him sitting with his head in his hands, gazing at the floor as if the riddle of his life lay there to be deciphered. About this time, too, he began to sing to himself very quietly in the shop.

Anna, bustling about overhead, caught an echo of it—a quaint, plaintive air.

> *"Oh, they call me 'Hanging Johnny'*
> *(Away, boys, away!)*
> *They say I hangs for money*
> *(Hang, boys, hang!)"*

It was always the same song, and it sounded very melancholy in the murky little shop with its old boots and shoes.

Once Anna stopped to listen, and heard the second verse.

> *"Oh, first I hanged my mother,"*

And the chorus a little louder:

> *"Away, boys, away!*
> *My sister and my brother—"*

She ran to the top of the stairs:
"Johnny, don't sing that, I don't like it."

Perhaps it was because she was tired of the sorrowful air, but the song got on her nerves—if indeed she had any—unpleasantly. For that was a side of Johnny's life she had never pried into. When he went away for an execution, she got all his things ready, and hurried him into the train, which he seemed determined to miss. She had particularly nice food for him when he came back, and she missed him incredibly during his absence, but she never asked him about any of his experiences, and he scarcely ever mentioned them. Anna did not waste her time reading the newspapers, so she was not the least interested in murderers or their trials. She respected Johnny's craving for secrecy about his profession as another of "his ways." She could not see that what he dreaded was not so much ridicule and hatred, as contempt. The people he belonged to despised an executioner, because he was felt to be carrying out the detested law of England, and Johnny was ashamed to face them with such an occupation. But he could not resign his post even if he wanted to—the fascination was too strong.

Anna had no hand in his affairs as executioner. He managed them quite well all by himself.

She wondered very occasionally how a man like Johnny could ever have taken up this calling, but she supposed "they" found him satisfactory, or they would have dismissed him.

One Wednesday he closed the shop early and went for a walk in the rain.

Anna was annoyed by this, but when he came upstairs with the water running off his coat in rivulets, she hurried to him full of anxious solicitation.

"Johnny, come in and get warm. You're soaked to the skin."

He went instantly to his usual place by the fire, and a thin steam arose from his clothes.

"Oh, Johnny," she protested, "don't sit by the fire, wet. Go and change, and when you come back I'll have a cup of tea for you."

"Let me be, can't you," he said irritably. "I'm after walking three hours. I want to rest."

But she was eager to see him comfortable and tidy, drinking the strong, hot tea.

"Now get up, Johnny," she said shaking him by the arm. "I have your other coat laid out on the bed. Don't be sitting there, catching your death of cold. Go on now, and don't be vexing."

A slow colour crept into his face and up the low, white forehead.

"Woman, will you never leave me alone? There's no peace in this house at all."

The words hurt her a little, and she flushed too.

"That's a nice way to talk," she said, "and me doing all I can to make you comfortable—"

He looked up and saw the puzzled look in her eyes. In a moment his arms were round her waist.

"Anna, I'm sorry. You're the best girl a man ever had. Kiss me, Anna, and then sit on my knee and we'll talk secrets?"

But her body did not respond to the wistful hunger of his arms. She stiffened a little, and began to pin up a loose braid of hair.

"I have a herring in the pan for you," she said brightly. "I know they're what you like best of all."

The light in Johnny's eyes went out, and his habitual heavy frown came down on his forehead.

"Food, food!" he muttered, "that's all you do be thinking of. Food and keeping the place clean. Sure, what's the good of them things to me, when all I want—"

He paused almost fearfully, but Anna's hot temper blazed out. "Is that what you're saying and me trying to make you comfortable? I work my fingers to the bone for you and what do you ever do but sit and gape at nothing like an idiot? Tell me that?"

"And who asked you to work your fingers to the bone? Sure, what do I care if the floor is clean or if it's not clean? You think I'll be content with a herring and a swept floor and not a bit of anything else at all."

"Well, no one's asking you to eat the herring," snapped Anna. "I won't get another for you again in a hurry."

Then Johnny suddenly seemed to grow calm. Anna, used to people who lost their tempers hotly and found them the minute after, did not sense the beginnings of violent passion in his low voice.

"You're keeping my child away from me, Anna—"

But she rushed in again with reasoning and argument.

"Arrah, Johnny, have sense—"

He lost control of himself. "O God, have mercy!" he flung up his clenched hands. In a lower voice: "Where is Michael now?"

"Playing below in the shop," she said.

He strode away from her, but, at the door, he turned and looked back.

She was standing by the fire with a wondering look in her fine, dark eyes.

Johnny gave a hoarse cry and rushed back to her, falling, grovelling almost at her feet.

He moaned despairingly. "Oh, I love you so, I love you so!"

She tried to pull away the arms that clung frantically round her waist, but their grip was too fierce. Then she wondered if he were going mad, and she grew frightened.

"Johnny, leave go!" she cried, beating the bent black head with her hands. "You're hurting me. You've never behaved like this before. Oh, the fish is burning. I smell it. Leave go of me at once."

His arms dropped from her quite slowly, and he raised his head. His eyelids were inflamed, and he looked rather dazed and miserable.

Without saying another word to her, he opened the door and tramped down the stairs to the shop.

Anna moved the pan of burnt fish, angry at the waste of good food. But her face was troubled.

"I do hope Johnny's not sickening for anything," her thoughts ran. "He might well be, indeed, going out in the rain without his thick coat. If he ever goes on like this again, I'll have him see the doctor."

Suddenly she heard Michael scream—a frightened hurt scream.

She put down the pan and rushed headlong down the stairs. The shop door was open, and the gusts of rain and wind had put the candle out.

"Michael," she called.

"Here I am," he came to her, sobbing a little.

"What's the matter with you? Where's daddy?"

"Gone out," he murmured sulkily.

She looked out at the dreary street with the wind howling like a mad thing round the houses. Raindrops spluttered fiercely in the puddles and raced along the gutters in miniature torrents.

Shivering a little, Anna closed the door.

"How silly of daddy. He's been so queer to-night. What are you crying for, Michael?"

"Because he hit me," said the child, whimpering.

"Hit you!" her eyes blazed.

"He said would I come out with him in the rain, and I said I must ask you, like you said."

"Good boy! And then?"

"He said did you tell me to say that, and I said 'yes!' and then he was awful angry and smacked me and ran out."

"The man's mad," said Anna. "I don't know what's come to him at all." She paused irresolutely, but Michael again claimed her attention.

"Mother, what's that burning smell?"

"It's fish I had for daddy." Her face softened suddenly. "Michael, go upstairs and get me my shawl. I've sixpence on me and I'll run out to the shops and get two herrings for daddy. He'll he glad of them when he gets home. Poor Johnny. The Lord send he isn't going to be ill."

Chapter XVI

After this, Michael got into the habit of stealing down to the shop during the daytime, when Anna was too busy to notice him.

He found his daddy a charming companion.

Daddy had strange, enthralling things to show him and tell him. He could not quite understand all daddy's explanations about people being hanged, but he found it very interesting.

"You see, there's a big cross beam with hooks fastened into it to hold the rope," Johnny said. "And there are two thick doors hung on long hinges that I put resting on an iron draw bar. Then I pull the lever one way, and that moves the draw bar the other way, so that the hinges drop through the openings, and down go the big doors and there's a pit underneath them. Bring your doll now, and I'll show you."

Michael had a figure that Johnny had made out of rags and painted the face with red ink. It was a grotesque thing, but it was Michael's inseparable companion.

It was a willing victim, and it was hanged realistically, a miniature scaffold being contrived by Johnny.

Another day, Michael would be shown the rope that had really hanged people, and the leather straps that pinioned their arms and legs.

"There's a white cap like a bag I pull over the faces of them," said Johnny. "That's when we go through the prison yard, where they dig the graves. It would be an awful thing to see your grave ready for you, knowing they'd be shovelling the earth over you that same evening, and the quick lime eating up your body."

"Do you see this stain, now?" Johnny said once, pointing to a dull mark on his rope. "That's the blood of Donal Leary who beat his wife to death. Drunk or mad he was at the time, I'd take my oath, but that never came up at all in the court. An *omadhaun* of a doctor—bad scran to him—made me give him a drop that I knew well enough was too long for him, him being a small fellow, not big enough, you'd be thinking, to thrash the life out of a woman. Well, when the drop fell down, I saw the rope jerk up, and there was the poor man lying at the bottom of the pit with the head of him jerked off his shoulders, and lying beside him."

Michael was frightened, not so much by the story as by the horror in his father's voice. Johnny had never got rid of the shocked memory, and the child caught an echo of it, here in the dusty cobwebbed little shop.

Once Johnny showed him his most precious thing "next to you." Michael stared, rather disappointed, at the piece of old, charred rope that Johnny took from his pocket.

"I wouldn't give this, if you offered me a rope of golden sovereigns twice the length of it, by way of exchange," he said.

"Is there magic in it, daddy?"

Johnny looked at it for a long time. Then he put it back in his pocket.

"I wouldn't say but there's something," he said. "I want it put in the coffin with me when I die."

"There's mother calling us for dinner," Michael remarked.

He had a strain of materialism in him, inherited from Anna.

"Well, sonny," Johnny said, "don't be telling your mother the things I do be saying to you down here. It's likely, now, she'd scold us for it, by reason of her not being able to understand."

"She'd do that," agreed Michael wisely. "Isn't it queer, daddy, the way she doesn't like to see me playing with the doll you made me. She says it's wasting my time I am, fooling with them things."

"Well now, a doll is great company," said Johnny. "If I was going on a journey, I'd rather have a doll with me than nobody at all. It's a terrible thing to be lonely."

But that night Michael screamed in his sleep, and, when Anna woke him, muttered something about a man's head being jerked off by a rope.

Partly because her sound sleep had been disturbed, Anna rebuked Johnny rather sharply the next morning.

"Have you no more sense than to be telling stories like that to the child—frightening the life out of him?" she added.

Johnny looked up at her sullenly.

"You're to stay here in this room, Michael," she said. "I won't have you interrupting your daddy at his work."

Michael burst into tears at this sentence, but Johnny said not a word of comfort.

As he went into the shop, which would be very lonely without the small presence he had loved to see there, he muttered to himself: "She's taking the child away from me."

That day was memorable. Anna set it down afterwards as the beginning of everything.

She had just finished washing up the supper things, and was taking her interminable darning out of her basket. Johnny sat as usual, gazing into the fire. He never smoked a pipe, and Anna, who liked men to have men's habits, often wished he would.

"What's that?" she said suddenly, raising her head.

Someone was knocking at the shop door, knocking loudly and anxiously. She glanced to Johnny, then, knowing it would take longer to rouse him than to go herself, she took the key from its hiding-place and went down the stairs.

She could hear the rain falling outside as she unlocked the door. A gust of wind rushed in and went shrieking through the shop. Someone stood outside, wrapped in a long, dark garment that blew out on either side of him like wings.

"What do you want?" said Anna.

The moon suddenly forced a rift in the clouds, and the light showed her a white, emaciated face, with eyes that looked like black holes bored into it.

"Will you let me come in," said the stranger. "I'm wet through with the rain."

Anna had a very curious instinct to shut the door in his face, but she was charitable, and she would not listen to it.

"You can shelter here," she said. "Let me shut the door, for the place is getting soaked."

As they went up the steep, wooden stairs, she asked over her shoulder: "You've had a long walk?"

"Walking the streets," he said, "walking the streets of the city. It's a bitter night and all the people are deaf."

With certain misgivings Anna opened the door of the upper room.

"You can come in here," she said. Then she caught her breath with surprise, for the candle light revealed him as a priest. He was clothed in a wide, black cassock which was dripping with water. His head was bare.

As the door opened, Johnny looked up and all the blood left

his lips.

The priest took a step forward.

"Hanging Johnny!" he said.

Johnny bent his head and did not speak.

"God led me to you," said the priest. "You have not laid your rope down, Johnny Cregan. I smell the blood on your hands."

"I got to live," Johnny muttered sullenly. "Damn it, haven't I got to live?"

Anna had listened in amazement.

"Johnny, what's all this?" she broke in. "I don't understand."

The priest turned very slowly and looked at her.

"That is my wife," said Johnny in a low voice.

"Did you buy that with the money?" asked the priest, pointing with a starved finger to the dresser, the most conspicuous bit of furniture in the room.

"What money?" said Anna.

"The money they give your husband for hanging God's victims."

"I don't know what you mean," she said. "If it's the money Johnny earns as a hangman, I bought this whole house out of it, and I'm saving it all now to buy a respectable place out of these slums. Is that all you want to know?"

Her tone was openly hostile, for she disliked the look of him, and she saw that Johnny, for some strange reason, was afraid of him.

"She is another enemy," said the priest. "She is deaf, like all the others."

"How dare you say that! I've got perfectly good hearing—"

"Woman, be silent," he said and turned impatiently away from her. Anna was outraged and furiously indignant, but the words died on her tongue before the strong, compelling power in his eyes.

"How did you come here?" whispered Johnny. "Tell me about it all."

"I resigned after they murdered poor Tim Derrybawn. I have been walking the country, walking the country. The Spirit of God will not let me rest." His voice became sterner. "Johnny Cregan, did the words I spoke to you by Tim Derrybawn's body on the scaffold mean nothing to you at all?"

Johnny drooped his head, and the hunted, miserable expression crept again into his eyes.

"Leave us, woman!" said the priest to Anna.

She set her hands on her hips.

"I'm not afraid of you! Trying to drive an honest woman from her own fireside—"

But his eyes were on her and she felt herself going to the door, her legs moving as if they were clockwork and not directed by her own will. For a long time she stayed down in the shop listening to the voices in the room above.

The priest spoke a great deal. His voice sometimes rose to a frenzied scream and sank again to a hoarse muttering.

"He can say what he likes," she thought to herself. "I won't go into the room again while he's there."

And, as a compensation, she lit the candle and began to dust the shop, shaking the spiders out of their lairs in the ceiling and under the counter with her merciless duster.

Johnny always protested angrily against any attempt to clean the shop, but she thought how pleased he would be to come down in the morning and find it orderly and neat, with his things nicely arranged for him.

In the farther corner, where the shadows were very black and dusty, lay Johnny's sack where he still kept his rope and straps. She did not touch this.

Her dislike of the priest upstairs had grown into a vague uneasiness, and she sought relief in physical action, as some people do.

Presently she heard steps on the stairs.

Thanks be to God, he was going.

For some reason, she stayed quietly in her dark corner, as Johnny opened the door. The candle on the counter threw distorting shadows over the priest's face.

He stood in the doorway, with one arm upraised, like an immense, evil shadow, and above the fury of wind and rain his voice rang out:

"You are drawing God's curse down on you."

Johnny went upstairs again, and his footsteps sounded very weary and hopeless.

Anna found him crouched over the fire, his head held in his two hands.

"Johnny," she said, "who was that queer man?"

"Father Gilligan," said Johnny. "He that was chaplain in the prison where I hanged Tim Derrybawn—God rest his soul."

"What did he behave so oddly for?"

"I never thought to see him again. Oh, it's a sinful beast of a man I am, and not fit to be in the room with him—a man of God."

"Will you stop your nonsense, Johnny," said Anna, exasperated, "and tell me what he spoke like that to you for? It's no business of his if you were a murderer, instead of an honest executioner, who earns his pay with working honestly for it."

Johnny glanced up at her. She looked very solid and dependable as she stood in front of him, her arms folded over her well-developed chest. In his own delicate, diffident way, he tried to make her understand.

"You see, Anna, it was a great sin I did in the days before I come to your village. Tim Derrybawn, that they thought shot Peter Connor in the Green Fire Club at Daly's, was my friend, the only friend I had in the town where they hated me. And I hanged him. It's like murder on my soul. I wish to God I'd let them have me up in Court for the debts I owed before I touched Tim with a rope." He let his face sink on his hands, and Anna made an effort to console him.

"Well, it wasn't your fault Tim Derrybawn was innocent. I remember hearing about the case now. No one was to blame, and I always think it is clever of the judge to make so few mistakes in finding out the people that do the murders."

He saw how completely she had missed his point, but he did not try to argue with her.

"And what had the priest to do with it?" she persisted, starting on her belated darning very briskly to make up for lost time.

"Ah, the priest!" Johnny shuddered and bent over the fire as if a sudden coldness had come on him.

Chapter XVII

When Father Gilligan walked through the slums, all the children fled, screaming, away from him. He walked very fast, his black cassock blown about in the wind, but what frightened the children was the way he muttered to himself, always muttered, muttered things that no one must ever try to hear. The mothers made the most of this: "If you don't stop your bawling," they said to the children when they were naughty, "Father Gilligan will come and take you away." But they were really a little frightened themselves, and they used to cross themselves when he passed by, for fear there was enchantment in his eyes and his white, skeleton face.

Everyone knew that he was mad—quite mad.

"There's no reason in him at all," some of the women said compassionately to each other; "it's a great pity now to see a man not right in his head, and he a priest." Father Gilligan passed often through the slums on his way to the cobbler's shop in St. Brigid Street. Johnny would look up and see his tall, bony figure stooping in the doorway.

He would speak to Johnny for hours, his eyes blazing and fanatical, and tell him terrible things. Johnny was very miserable and terrified in those days, but he clung to the priest, because he was the only one who could protect him from the fury of God.

"What does the mad priest be saying to your husband, Mrs.

Croghan?" inquired Mrs. Carey, who was wild with curiosity.

"The priest? Johnny hasn't seen him since."

"Pardon me, ma'am," said Mrs. Carey triumphantly, "I've watched every day, for the last week, and I've seen him come to the shop every day, without missing a day. He does be talking to your husband hours at a time, so he does. If it was Danny who was colloguing with him I'd not let him be for a minute, till I got it out of him what it is the priest says."

Anna looked sharply at Johnny that day, and saw that his cheeks were sunken and his eyes looked "queer." They were haunted eyes, but she could not have realised that. Then something happened that made her see vaguely what the priest had done to Johnny.

"I left my scissors down in the shop," she said to him after supper, "will you go and fetch them?" Johnny scowled and muttered something, but Michael called out: "Daddy's afraid of the dark. He's afraid to be alone in the dark."

"Hold your tongue," said Johnny fiercely. He flung the door open, and went downstairs, shutting it after him. But as he came up again she heard his feet almost tripping over each other in their haste to reach the lighted room again. She looked searchingly at him when he came in. Then she asked frankly: "Has Father Gilligan been talking to you lately, Johnny?"

"Why wouldn't he be talking to me?" he said sullenly.

"Well, I wouldn't listen to him. He's only a mad creature with no sense in him."

"Mad!" cried Johnny. "Who are you to be saying that about a man of God? Sure, don't the Saints themselves come and whisper to him and him asleep?"

She dropped her work and stared at him in amazement.

"Is that what he says to you, Johnny?"

"Why are you laughing?" he said angrily. "It's terrible things they tell him. Things that would frighten the heart out of you."

She gazed hard at him to see if he really believed it. Then her robust, clear laughter rang out: "Why, the child there wouldn't swallow those stories. I wonder, sometimes, if you're all there, Johnny, the way you waste your time listening to the talk of a madman."

He scowled and flushed under her contempt, hut she could not shake his belief.

He was utterly untaught and very superstitious. He accepted Father Gilligan's talk of the flaming fires that yawned under his feet because he had aided the vengeance of men as gospel truth, and it terrified him. And Anna laughed at him.

His mentality was like a very delicate, rare flower, and she was crushing it under the feet of her materialism. But she was anxious about him, because she knew he was not well, so she tried to cheer him by taking him to look at the shops.

It was coming near Christmas, and they were all gaily lighted up. Johnny took no interest in them. He walked along, his eyes bent along the ground and scarcely spoke a word.

"What do you want me to give you for Christmas?" asked Anna, trying to attract his attention.

"I don't care a damn."

The rudeness of this hurt and surprised her. It was so terribly unlike Johnny.

But as they passed a rather pretentious shop, with many desirable things in the window, he suddenly clutched her arm and pointed.

"I want that," he cried.

It was a man's immense silk handkerchief, made of fifty different shades that all seemed to blend with one another in an entrancing pattern.

"I wouldn't like to see you with that in your pocket," said Anna in horror. "It's like what an actor would wear. Besides, it's much too dear."

"You never see what's beautiful," he said hotly. It was marked seven-and-six, and he gazed yearningly at it. He had a passion for colour and beauty, and the gawdy thing satisfied it. The drab surroundings of his life had made the passion rather crude and untamed.

"If you want a handkerchief," said Anna, "there's a nice dark blue one, and it's only two shillings."

"It's the coloured one I want. We could take the money for it out of the drawer."

"Our savings! Johnny, what are you thinking of!"

He stamped his foot.

"Oh!" he said, "it drives me mad to be scraping along, scraping along the way we do, never buying anything beautiful, when there's all that money in the drawer of the dresser."

"Johnny!" She was astonished and shocked. "You know why we can't spend that money."

"I do not, then. We'll be as poor again after we buy the big place you do be talking of. It's my money, Anna, why should you keep it from me?"

He had never spoken like this to her, and she was going to be angry with him. But instead, she felt pitying, because there was a choke in his voice.

"Would it make you happy, Johnny, if I bought it for you?"

"Yes—yes," he said.

So she bought it and gave it to him, consoled for the emptiness of the purse by the radiant lighting up of his face. But it could not make him happy. Fear tortured him and, though Anna tried to help him, she laboured in ignorance. The shadow of Father Gilligan hung very heavily over the cobbler's shop in St. Brigid Street.

Chapter XVIII

Anyone walking up St. Brigid Street, and turning a corner on the right would have found himself in the street of the Three Marys. Here there was a large, tall house with dirty windows. A sign swung over the door, with "The Star" painted on it in faded gilt letters.

Neil Fogarty was the proprietor of "The Star," and he and his pub were the centre of much gossip.

One night he stood before the fire, keeping the heat from the company with his great body. For he was a large, fleshy man and well-fed. He had a handsome face, and his hair was dark and rather oily.

His clothes were very smart. He wore a red and gold tie, and two rings with big glass stones in them. A mauve handkerchief, picked out in red and gold to match the tie, was fastened round his waist.

When there was a pause in the conversation, he jingled some money in his pocket, or consulted a watch on the end of a very bright gold chain.

But there were few lulls in the medley of voices and clinking glasses.

There were about twenty people in the room—all men, except three old women who smoked pipes. It was a large room, and there had once been pink, floral paper on the walls, which was now peeling off in strips.

Six guttering candles supplied the light, only half revealing the dust and cobwebs, and the fat black spiders that lived in the corners never disturbed by a broom.

A door at one end led into a card-room, and there were some other rooms where there were younger women. It was a very superior public-house.

The evening had not really started, and there had only been enough political opinions hurled about for Ned Cleary to be kicked out of the house, and Joe Mullen to be knocked unconscious by someone's fist.

Just after this happened, a door at one side of the room opened, and a small, drab woman crept in. Her face was very dirty and pale, and she had quite colourless hair that hung round her ears, some shreds being still retained by hairpins. She wore a faded shawl, and a skirt that was torn across the hem. She had black cotton stockings, and odd slippers, both being made for the right foot, that slipped up and down, making her heels bleed through the holes in her stockings.

"Is Neil here?" she said, blinking in the smoky atmosphere.

Neil Fogarty pulled her over to him and whispered fiercely: "How dare you come in here dressed like that? I'll have the heart out of you for it, shaming me in front of my friends."

She quailed before him, because she thought he was going to strike her. But instead, he spoke very loudly and brutally. "Now, aren't those the lovely stockings she's wearing! Look at the elegant gown that's in it! Maybe that gap is all in the latest fashion."

The woman stood quite quiet while he jeered and pointed, his face a dull scarlet.

Suddenly he seized her by the shoulder and pushed her to the door.

"If you ever come here again looking like that," he hissed at her, "I'll kick the entrails out of you."

When she had gone, he plunged into loud, reckless conversation with a man at a distant table.

He liked to impress his guests with his wealth and his imitation of the "quality." And he had been disgraced, but he would not show them that he cared. Boldly he challenged the glances of all the eyes in the room, and they dropped before his defiant, scowling gaze.

The woman herself was slopping along a dark stone passage till she reached the kitchen in the basement.

Here was a filthy, littered floor and a smelly sink, round which piles of glasses and plates waited to be washed.

She looked at these helplessly, then she stared about for a cloth. Not finding one, she took off her stocking, dipped it in the greasy water, and began, vaguely and unmethodically, to wipe the plates with it, setting them aside, some with the remains of gravy stiffening on them, to dry as best they might.

Chapter XIX

Johnny had to go to Wexford for an execution. Anna prepared everything, and he made no protest. As he went out of the house, he said to her:

"This is the last time." That was all.

He was away four days, and the time passed very slowly with Anna.

"Wouldn't it be awful," said little Michael, "if daddy never came back at all? Or if he fell out of the train and got smashed?"

"Don't talk nonsense," said Anna sharply. She realised in the lonely days without Johnny how very much he meant to her.

"He'll bring back a coat for himself, maybe," she remarked to Michael, "and something perhaps that I could cut down for you. He brought a good pair of boots from the last execution."

On the fourth day Johnny came back. He looked very tired, and he flung himself straight into a chair and leaned his head back. Anna put a cushion behind his shoulders, and prepared a cup of tea. Michael climbed on his knee.

"What was it like, daddy? Was the man brave?"

"Oh, don't make me talk about it. It was raining as we went to the scaffold. I was glad of that. The world wouldn't seem so pleasant to him in the rain."

"Leave your dad alone, Michael," said Anna. "He is tired out."

A few hours later she asked him:

"Did they give you any of the man's clothes this time, Johnny?"

"They did. The fools."

"Where are they, then? I want to see if there's anything would do Michael."

He flushed in his peculiar, slow way and got to his feet.

"I flung them on the ground when they gave them to me. Is it let my child wear the clothes of a man I killed? If I put a stitch that man had worn on myself, it would prick me to death, because I hanged him."

"Oh, Johnny, it's a great fool of a man you are," she said with annoyance. "Michael's badly in need of a new pair of breeches, and yourself of a new coat, and you go throwing away good clothes, like as if you were a lord."

Johnny clenched his hands as though she maddened him.

"Oh, you have no understanding," he said and went into the bedroom.

The next morning Father Gilligan came again to the shop. He was shaking with fury.

"Do you not believe the words I tell you?" he screamed to Johnny. "Do you laugh at me like the others?"

"What do you mean, Father?"

"Did you think I would not know that you went on Wednesday to hang a man? Oh, I cannot understand how brutes and fools like you can deliberately challenge the anger of God!" The words choked him, and he lifted his distorted, maniacal face to heaven.

"Your reverence—" pleaded Johnny.

"You wanted the money. Money, money, that's all you think of. I wonder why it did not burn your fingers off. Oh, you fool, you fool, I wish the Lord would hurl you this moment into the fire that waits for you under your feet."

He was so terrible, that Johnny clutched his robe in an agony of fear. "That was my last execution, your reverence. I won't touch a rope ever again."

His remorse soothed the priest a little.

"Explain it to me all again, Father," pleaded Johnny, "the way I can understand it once and tor all."

Father Gilligan brought his own distraught mind down to the level of this primitive, sensitive one.

"Day by day while I walk the streets, God speaks to me. He does not wish murderers to be killed. The taking of life is filth in His sight, but He will work out His own revenge on the people that do murder. Death is a puny, useless punishment. The Lord would punish each man according to his crime and the circumstances that made him do it. Our law often gives the same penalty to the man that kills a child out of lust and cruelty, and the man that kills his wife because she drove him to it out of jealousy and rage. Do you not see how the Lord would consider these things?

"We have tried hanging for hundreds of years. Has it made fewer crimes, fewer murderers? No! Then why shall we not trust a while in the Judgment of God?

"The Lord has summoned me to go out into the world, and collect a band of prophets who will preach this great truth to mankind. When everyone knows it, there will be no more murder on earth. Those who do not fear death will learn to fear the punishments of God. That is my mission. The people are fools who laugh and mock, and it is very hard for me, but the Lord helps me, and I will go on till I die."

Johnny listened, his eyes troubled and afraid.

"I'll resign," he said quickly. "I'll not have any more to do with the work I've taken up."

"You will do well," said Father Gilligan. He had spoken quite calmly, but the flame still lurked in his eyes, ready to blaze up at any moment.

"God is angry with the men who punish murderers," he said. "His curse hangs over each of them, and over you above all of them, Johnny Cregan, because of the hateful and degrading work you have done."

Johnny glanced fearfully into the dark corners of the shop. His diseased imagination conjured up more frightful things than Father Gilligan described.

"Will it not be enough if I resign my job?" he asked anxiously.

"That will not be enough."

"What must I do, then, your reverence?"

But the priest knew that the time had not come yet to tell him what else would be required of him. Instead, he studied him for a while in silence. Then he asked abruptly: "Are you happy, Johnny Cregan?"

The cobbler's head was bent low over a shoe he was stitching.

"Happy?" he muttered. "No, I'm not happy."

"You have a home."

"It's a sad home to me," said Johnny. "There's no comfort in it at all. It's all clean and hard like a stone with no friendliness or warmth anywhere. It's little my wife cares for me or for anything."

He had spoken in a low voice, but with a kind of sullen passion like a mutiny against his fate.

"There is your child," said the priest gently.

"The child? She's wiling him away from me." He struggled, choking, to his feet.

"They have me driven mad in this place," he whispered.

Anna heard with dismay his announcement that he was going to resign his post of executioner.

"Johnny, you can't. We've nearly got enough money now for the big shop, and you can't give up just when we're wanting about thirty pounds more."

Johnny did not reply. How could he convey Father Gilligan's terrible message to her narrow understanding?

"When we leave this place," she went on, "you can resign. I don't know as I'd like you to be a hangman when we've got the grocery shop. We want to he really respectable then, and send Michael to school."

"I will resign now," said Johnny. He stood up, and a little of Father Gilligan's fanaticism seemed to burn in his eyes. "Would you be going against the command of God? He has written for us all to read"—his voice grew awed and fearful—"'Vengeance is Mine. I will repay.'"

"My curse on that mad priest, who's got hold of Johnny," fumed Anna inwardly. As a good Catholic, she had never read the Bible, but a sudden memory of hearing that quotation discussed flashed into her mind.

"Johnny!" she said triumphantly. "He said that to the Jews. You're not a Jew."

"Is it the Jews? Well, now, I must tell that to—"

He did not say the name, but she was satisfied, for he began to help Michael with his bricks and was happier that evening than she had known him for weeks.

But it could not last, for he soon grew morose and nervous again.

He began to go out in the evenings, not returning till late, and Anna was anxious and worried because she knew he was down in the wee, wooden hut by the river, listening to Father Gilligan preach.

Chapter XX

One night Johnny was tramping home after a visit to Father Gilligan. Snow was falling, and he shivered in his threadbare clothes. Only his head was burning hot with the excitement the priest always awoke in him. He walked by a roundabout road, mechanically swinging his arms to get warm, and presently found himself in the street of the Three Marys.

"Is it yourself that's in it?" a voice shouted suddenly in his ear, and someone slapped his shoulder.

Johnny's nerves were so much on edge that he jumped and gave a stifled cry. But it was only Danny Carey.

"You frightened me," said Johnny. The other man laughed.

"It's a cruel night," he said. "Is it likely, now, you'd come into Fogarty's and have a drop of something with me?"

The snow was falling heavily, and Johnny's teeth chattered in his head. Anna would be in bed now and the fire would be out. He was tired, but lately he had not been able to sleep. The nights meant long hours of misery and terror.

"I'll come," he said recklessly.

Danny Carey took him by the arm and led him to a large house, the windows of which were all lit up. When they opened the door a draught of heavenly, warm air rushed out to greet them like a welcome.

The taproom was very full, but there was one seat near the fire which they commandeered at once. Neil Fogarty stood as usual with his back to the fire, and they were so near him that they caught at intervals whiffs of his scent and hair oil. Johnny's spirits rose in the warm air and the comfort of humanity all around him.

He began to talk, and his eyes shone.

Once or twice he laughed and then his face was so beautiful that it seemed to belong to another world. The haunted, haggard expression had lifted itself for the time.

Presently a door opened, and the slatternly, drab woman came in. She seemed to drift aimlessly across the room, until she reached a table very near Johnny. One of the men began to talk to her, and she leaned over to him and laughed.

Neil Fogarty turned and saw, and his fullblooded face grew purple.

He strode to the table and dealt the man a blow with his clenched fist. The man's head fell back and he rolled sideways off the bench.

"That'll teach you to leave my wife alone," said Neil Fogarty.

He seized the woman by the arm.

"Get out of this, you dirty-livered little bitch," he snarled. Then he added a few words so softly that only Johnny heard them. It was something so obscene and cruel that Johnny's manhood and chivalry rose within him.

He leaped up and swung the little creature out of Fogarty's grasp.

Then his hand flew up and Fogarty went reeling backwards from a sharp blow on the mouth.

There was a gasp from the onlookers, and someone shouted. Cursing with fury, Neil Fogarty struggled to his feet and lunged at Johnny again and again.

In the grip of his brute strength, Johnny was helpless. Blow after blow was showered on his face and body, and he was not strong enough to put up any resistance.

Of course, by this time everyone was fighting. The whole room was a medley of shouting and groaning. Men rushed in from other rooms and flung themselves with fierce delight into the tumult.

Johnny felt Neil Fogarty torn off him, and he began to struggle through the swirling mass of humanity to the door.

He found it at last, and stumbled into the street. But he could not walk. Every part of him throbbed with agony. He leant against the house and blood poured from his nose.

Suddenly he felt a hand laid on his arm. He looked down and saw the woman.

"What did you do that for?" she asked in her low, tired voice.

"What did I do it for?" He stared at her in amazement.

"Couldn't you see he wasn't hurting me?"

"But, didn't you—didn't you mind what he said?" Johnny stammered a little, for the thing Neil Fogarty had said was very horrible.

She pushed the hair off her forehead with a weary, drab gesture.

"Suppose I'm used to it. We've been married ten years."

A protective feeling came suddenly over Johnny. She was so small and starved, and in the snow her face looked pinched and cold.

"Has he ever hurt you?" he asked.

"He does sometimes, I'm afraid then. He can kick mighty hard."

The wild cries and tumult inside the house came faintly to Johnny's ears. Suddenly a shot rang out, and they heard someone throw the candles down. The darkness produced instant silence.

"I'd best be going in," said Neil Fogarty's wife. She moved away, but Johnny caught her skinny little arm.

"Wait now. Can I come sometimes and see you, Mrs. Fogarty? Will you let me?"

"You couldn't do that. Neil would beat me like hell—"

An interested crowd, drawn by the fighting in the house, had begun to collect on the pavement.

"Couldn't you manage it the way he'd not know?" pleaded Johnny. He did not quite know why he was insisting. Something in him was strongly drawn to the little creature.

She came close to him.

"Your nose is bleeding," she said in a whisper, "you got hurt because of me. If you come round to the back of the house sometimes, you'll see a bit of rag in my window, and you'll know you can come up to me without fear of Neil."

Then she wriggled out of his grasp like a little eel and ran away through the snow.

Chapter XXI

When Anna awoke in the morning she saw that Johnny, instead of lying awake with wipe open eyes staring into space, was in a heavy sleep. His hair was tangled round his face, and there was a great bruise on his forehead.

His upper lip was cut and there were stains of blood round his nose.

As she gazed at him he slowly opened his eyes, lifted his head and let it fall back heavily on the pillow.

"Johnny, what has happened to you?" she gasped.

He did not answer and threw his arm across his forehead as though to hide the bruise from her.

"Did you go to Father Gilligan last night?"

"Yes," he murmured sulkily.

Anna threw off the blankets and sprang vigorously out of bed. Johnny did not move.

When she was half dressed she bent over him. "Johnny, why don't you cut away from that madman and have done with it?"

"You don't know what you're saying." His voice grew lower, "He's a good man—the only man who can save me from the curse."

"The curse?" she echoed.

He held out his hand.

"Do you see the way that shakes? May be 'tis the beginning

of it."

She caught the hand and held it close to her, in an effort to still the dreadful pang that had gone through her heart when she heard him talk like a lunatic.

"Johnny," she said, "I'm not going to let Father Gilligan come to this house anymore."

He looked up at her incredulously.

"You can't stop him. The likes of you."

"He can't come in if I lock the door in his face," she said simply.

"Anna, Anna, you can't do that. He'll put a curse on you, too."

"I'll just tell him he's not to come here anymore," she said, ignoring this. "It's my house and I won't have lunatics in it."

"Anna, for the love of God, don't talk like that."

She began to lose patience.

"I won't have him coming here anymore. He upsets you, Johnny, and it's not good for you to be keeping company with him. Oh, stop your talk about curses and Saints. I'm not afraid of that mad creature, I'm only sorry for him. It's a terrible misfortune on him."

Johnny went down to the shop, and Anna listened all the morning for the sound of that frenzied, thrilling voice. But Father Gilligan did not come.

"When he doesn't see the priest," Anna thought, "he'll not want to be going out at night to listen to him preaching. He'll get rid of all his queerness and we'll go on like we did before."

So she was very happy while she swept and dusted, and peeled the potatoes for dinner.

Mrs. Carey dropped in at twelve o'clock, full of excited news.

"Mrs. Croghan, ma'am, did you hear the fighting up at 'The Star' in the night?"

"I did not," said Anna coldly.

"Ah, your husband wouldn't tell you about it, I'll be bound," said Mrs. Carey, in the voice of the rejoicing scandal-monger.

"I don't suppose he knew anything of it," said Anna, busy with her potatoes.

"You're mistook then, for 'twas he started it all."

Anna turned sharply.

"What's that?" she cried.

"I had the whole story from Danny," began Mrs. Carey, delighted with her success. "Neil Fogarty's little bit of a woman started colloguing with Ted Leary—did you ever clap eyes on Ted Leary, ma'am?"

"I don't know him at all."

"The biggest rascal, saving your presence, between this and county Wicklow. Well, when Neil sees this, up he jumps and knocks Ted Leary over with a blow of his fist. Then he starts giving the woman a bit of his tongue, and nothing would do Johnny, when he hears this, but to stand up to Neil Fogarty and plant his fist on the red face of him.

"Well, ma'am, Neil was mad as a lion by reason of being knocked down by a bit of a gossoon, begging your pardon, like your husband. So he ups and give back as good as he got, and by thunder Johnny was lucky to get out of it as easy as he did. I seen the bruises on him when I come through the shop. Danny says Neil's wife was outside with him afterwards the best part of an hour."

Danny Carey had not made this statement, but his wife had the artist's delight in her story and added it as a finishing touch.

"I wish I'd known," said Anna, her eyes shining, "I'd have told him I was so proud of him. It was a brave thing to do. Poor Mrs. Fogarty! She's a dirty slut of a woman, but I can't help feeling sorry for her. It's a hard life he leads her—poor creature.

Mrs. Carey was bitterly disappointed.

"It's queer now, he never told you," she said, still trying to rouse the other woman to some feeling of jealousy.

"Oh, that's just like Johnny. He wouldn't like to be talking and boasting of how brave he was. I'm glad indeed he stood up for little Mrs. Fogarty. It's a great shame to see other men, stronger than Johnny, standing round doing nothing while that big brute of a man bullies her."

"It's not bullying her he'll be," retorted Mrs. Carey flushing, "it's the things he does be saying!"

"That's worse," said Anna, also flushing, because she did not like to think of the things a man like Neil Fogarty might say.

But she was very proud of Johnny. "That priest hasn't done him so much harm," she told herself, "he's still the fine man he was when I married him."

For she did not know that the Johnny she had married in the little stone chapel at Ballyboulteen had vanished for ever the first time she repulsed one of his caresses.

That evening she went out to buy some household things she had forgotten in the morning. Johnny had left the shop so she took her own key—they each had one—and locked the shop door. She returned in half an hour, her basket on her arm, and looking very trim and comely with her plaid shawl drawn over her head.

She was a clever housekeeper and she was pleased with the purchases she had made.

As she came down the street she saw Father Gilligan standing outside the door of the cobbler's shop. Twilight was falling, and there was something sinister about the dark figure, waiting like death to gain admittance into the house. She hurried forward and came up to him, just as he was stretching out a finger to rap on the door.

Without taking any notice of him, she produced her key and unlocked the door.

The priest followed every movement with his sunken, gleaming eyes.

Then he said quite politely:

"Good evening, Mrs. Cregan. May I come in? Your husband expects me."

"You had better not come in, your reverence. I don't think my husband is waiting for you."

He stepped back in amazement. Then a little spot in his eyes began to glitter.

"What do you mean, Mrs. Cregan?"

"I don't want you to come here anymore," said Anna steadily. "I'm sorry to be rude, but I must tell you plainly."

His face grew scarlet and passionate.

"You have no right to say that. Those words should come from your husband."

Anna stood in the doorway of the shop, its dusky gloom making a background for her strong young figure.

"It's Johnny I'm thinking of," she said. Suddenly she forgot to be dignified. "He's been so queer since he saw you first. Oh, I know you say terrible things to him. Things that frighten him."

"I tell him of the fiery sword that hangs over his head wherever he moves," said the priest. "The earth breaks under his feet, waiting to swallow him up. The anger of God is upon him! The anger of God is upon him!" His voice rose to a shriek, and he brandished his arms high above his head.

Anna wanted to speak and found herself tongue-tied. She knew nothing of hypnotism, but there was hypnotism in his stark, blazing eyes.

"But I come to save Johnny Cregan," he said hoarsely, "and I will save him in spite of you."

He thrust his white face close to her and she stepped backwards, instinctively afraid. Then the familiar, musty leathery smell of the shop—such a little thing as that—gave her courage in face of this thing she could not understand.

"You talk so silly," she said. "I don't know what you mean. An executioner's job is very respectable. A Government job. And I won't let you make Johnny give it up, just when we've saved nearly enough money for the grocery store."

"You have no understanding," he said. "Money, money, is everything to you. You would hurl Johnny into the fire of Hell with your own hands if you could get five shillings for his soul. You have no thoughts above that."

He pointed to her well loaded basket.

"You shan't see Johnny again," she said angrily. "If you think you can manage him better than his own wife, you'd better try, that's all."

She turned to go into the shop, but he clutched her arm so tightly that it hurt her.

"You are one of his temptations," he said through his teeth, "the sordid temptations of the flesh. You are trying to pull his body away from me. His body—the only part of him you can understand. You have no power over his soul, thank God. I will help him to stand against you and obey the word of God which comes to me in my dreams. And against me you cannot prevail."

Anna did not grasp the meaning of all he said, but he threw her a look that roused in her a hot resentment that was not exactly modesty. No man had ever made her feel like that before, and it hurt. So she said very cruelly and deliberately, trying to wound him as hard:

"And you are mad. Everyone says so."

"Mad?" It was a sharp cry. The divine frenzy died out of his eyes and they became wretched and almost appealing. Then he gave a yell of fury. "You try to wound with vile insults the chosen of God. It's not true, it's not true. Let God strike you down where you stand for saying that. Oh, you she-devil—"

Anna, really frightened, had banged the door in his face and turned the key. In the safety of the dark, stuffy little shop, she thought, "I must never let that creature get hold of Johnny again. He's so crazy that he might throw Johnny into the river one of these days. It's not safe to be with him." Her face suddenly brightened. "I know what I'll do. I'll make his home so nice for Johnny, he won't want to go out to that horrible man. I'll try not to worry him. I'll try to get along with him better. That will make him forget Father Gilligan, and he won't resign, and soon we'll buy the grocery shop, and never see this place again."

But the personality of the priest was still very real and terrible, and it seemed to overshadow this promised happiness, so she sank on her knees by the counter and prayed very simply and earnestly: "Please, God, help Johnny and me, for I do love him better than anything in the whole world."

The very next evening Anna, full of her new idea, lit the candles earlier than usual and kindled a blazing fire. Then a thought entered her head that made her redden and laugh.

It was such an utterly absurd idea—she could not conceive how she had thought of it. And yet—she glanced at the clock, Johnny would be down in the shop for another hour. There was actually time to do it. She went into the bedroom and took a large cardboard box from the bottom of the cupboard. She hesitated just a second before she lifted the lid; she had not opened it for three years. She raised the sheet of white paper that was inside, and there lay a white muslin frock with blue ribbons, fresh and beautiful and uncreased. Her wedding dress. The dress she had called her "best" in the far-off days at Ballyboulteen. She unfolded it and held it up, and if her mind was different she would have seen herself walking from the little chapel—a bride on her husband's arm.

"I couldn't have a wedding gown, but I put on my best. Do you like it?"

Her cheeks began to burn, and thankful that no one had seen how foolish she had nearly been, she hastily replaced the dress in the box.

But as she picked up the paper, something fell out of it. A black wooden box, with stripes and circles of different colours painted all over it. The paint was beginning to wear off.

Rather sadly she lifted the lid and put her nose inside, but the scent had quite gone out of it. Then something reckless caught hold of her, something that was not Anna Croghan at all. She took off the brown dress she was wearing, lifted out the dainty, beautiful white one, and put it on.

It was six years out of date, but she could not fight down a wave of delight that rushed over her when she saw how gracefully the flounced skirt fell round her.

There was a tiny mirror on the wall, which showed her part of the bodice if she jumped, and though it had grown a little tight for her, the effect was very pleasing. The sleeves reached to the elbows, leaving the rest of her firm, work-roughened arms bare.

"I do look nice," she thought. "Whatever will Johnny say? But my hair? It looks funny done like this with the frock. I must do something with it."

She pulled all her hairpins out and let her hair fall down in a cascade of coppery-tinted darkness. She studied herself in the mirror for the first time in many years, and a slow, wonderful exultation came over her.

"I look young," she marvelled to herself. "I'm not so old after all."

She began to arrange her hair very carefully, bringing out all the soft little curls.

When it was finished, she stared at her reflection in breathless amazement.

"Oh, *what* will Johnny say?" she whispered.

Then she tore herself away and went into the other room, walking very carefully lest she should stumble over her bottom flounce. Mechanically she picked up her basket of mending and put it down again.

"It would somehow spoil the dress," she told herself. So she sat down by the fire and waited.

Then she heard a step on the stairs. A sudden panic seized her and she got up to run into the bedroom. She could not let Mrs. Carey or the neighbours see her like this.

But the door opened before she could retreat, and Michael danced into the room.

"Mother, have you a hook? We're fishing for a sardine in the gutter. Don saw it swimming. Oh—" he lifted his eyes and saw the ashamed, embarrassed figure in the doorway.

"Mother, what have you got that dress on for?" Then she advanced defiantly, braving it out.

"I thought I'd like to wear it this evening for fun."

"Oh, you look so pretty. I never seen anyone so pretty." He

touched a blue rosette with appreciative fingers. "Are we going to have a party, mother?"

Anna knew it was absurd to feel pleased at his admiration—pleased and gratified—but she could not help it.

"There's no one coming except father!" she said, trying to sound casual.

"Daddy will love it. He'll be so glad to see you looking all lovely. Why don't you look like that always?"

She could not answer this, so she coloured and turned to the dresser.

"Here's your hook, Michael; but of course it wasn't a sardine you saw. Sardines are never alive; you buy them in tins."

"Don says they're fishes' babies." He took another long, approving look at her. "I won't tell daddy a word about you when I go down," he said. "We'll have it a big surprise for him."

Again that absurd delight. But she would not let herself feel it.

"Run along now, Micky," she ordered, trying to believe his admiration irritated her.

He studied her again with a rapt, grave pleasure that made him terribly like Johnny.

Then he marched to the door.

"I tell you what"—he made a magnificent promise—"if you swear to look just zackly the same to-morrow, I'll bring you that sardine for supper and you can have it all."

Anna went back to her chair by the fire. She felt odd and uncomfortable without anything to occupy her hands.

But she did her best to picture Johnny's slow joy and amazement when he came in and saw his bride waiting for him, his bride as he had seen her six years ago.

"He ought to be up soon now," she thought. "I wonder if he'll really be pleased. Oh, I can hardly wait."

She looked at the clock. There were only five minutes more. She was feeling as excited as if something tremendous was about to happen.

One moment she was afraid to let him see her, and the next, she was longing for him to come. "What will he say?"—her brain repeated incessantly—"What will he say?"

Then across her pleasure and her joyous anticipations went a cold, sullen noise.

The shop door had shut with a bang. She raised her head sharply. It was the wind. Johnny had not gone out. Surely, surely, Johnny had not gone out this evening without a word to her.

But there was a pattering of feet on the stairs, and Michael rushed in, breathless with sobs.

"Mother, mother, daddy's gone out. He'll never see our surprise now. I ran after him, but he pushed me away. He won't see our surprise now."

He flung himself on the floor and cried miserably and uncontrollably.

Anna felt the tears prick her own eyes. The disappointment was such a bitter one. Almost cruel enough to make her cry too. Then the something that had seized her and made her put that old dress on passed completely out of her.

"Get up now, Michael, and don't be a baby," she said almost roughly to the child.

She hurried into the bedroom and tore the frock off and bundled it into the box.

"The Lord be praised," she said to herself as she stood in her brown dress and scraped her hair back from her forehead. "The Lord be praised Johnny didn't come in and see me got up in that foolery. Whatever possessed me to do it! He'd have thought I'd gone mad."

Chapter XXII

The back of the public-house known incongruously as "The Star," was like a high, narrow, stone wall. There were no windows in it at all, except two belonging to the kitchen in the basement and a tiny one almost at the top of the house. Just underneath this small window was a green, wooden door. To reach this door you had to climb an iron staircase that had been built up the outside of the house, and was made safe by a rusty iron railing in place of banisters.

The street here was very quiet and deserted. The houses on both sides had their backs turned and, like "The Star," displayed very few windows. After leaving the shop, Johnny Croghan walked slowly along this street. It was growing very dark, and there were queer shadows everywhere. None of the houses had lights in the windows, and this made them look empty and sad.

Johnny examined the windows of all the houses, very carefully, for he had never before been round to the back of "The Star."

At last he reached the foot of the staircase, and looked hopefully upwards. The window above the green door was illuminated by the quivering, timid light of a candle, and a piece of wincey had been fastened to the sill and fluttered in the breeze.

"I can come," thought Johnny joyously. He would have been bitterly disappointed if none of the windows had displayed an inviting signal. He had thought of Mrs. Fogarty a great deal. He began to mount the steps. Some of them were broken and his foot slipped in the darkness. As he came near the top, it swayed and creaked under his weight.

But he reached the door safely, and rapped on it with his coat sleeve drawn over his knuckles because he hated the feel of the wood against them.

There was a slight noise inside, and then the door was opened and Mrs. Fogarty let him in. The room was very small and it smelt of candle grease and clothes. There was just a bed and a table and a chair in it. The mattress on the bed was falling sideways and two blankets were tangled together in a heap on it. The table was littered with garments—some of them had fallen on the floor—a cracked mirror and a candle stuck in its own drippings. On the chair was a plate with a chop hardening in stiffened grease.

"I'd best take in the rag," said Mrs. Fogarty in her toneless voice. "I wouldn't wonder but Neil would see it, and he'd be up here then in two hop skips of a lame beggar."

She opened the window, unfastened the piece of wincey, and blew her nose loudly in it. It was covered with grease stains and a few spots of blood.

"I got a cold," she said, slipping it into her sleeve.

Johnny could not utter a word. Her calm acceptance of his presence, her lack of excitement or embarrassment was amazing.

There was no spirit of adventure about her. In the candle-light she looked just a drab, tired, hopeless little woman. One side of her hair had come down and lay in a dusty mat on her shoulder, the other side was supported precariously on hairpins that stuck out over her ears.

But the grey pallor of her face under its coating of dirt struck him again with pity.

"It's very cold," she said. "In the evenings I roll myself in the blankets." She was wearing a thin shawl, but her arms were blue with cold.

She climbed on the bed and flung herself among the blankets. After a slight hesitation, Johnny sat down beside her.

"You see," she said simply, "this is my room. Neil gave it to me, when he wasn't wanting me in his room anymore. I was glad."

Then she lay back and closed her eyes. She took no more notice of him. She was just too tired to move.

Johnny let his eyes wander round the room. The squalor did not nauseate him, though the air came laden with filth to his delicate nostrils. He turned his head and looked at the woman beside him. She had very small hands, and they lay limp and inert. They were pale and grimy, with very long, black nails. Once or twice she gave a little cough.

"Mrs. Fogarty," said Johnny.

She unclosed her eyes and pushed the hair off her forehead. "What name is there on you, Mrs. Fogarty, besides that one?"

"Rosa," she said quite simply.

"There's a pretty name for you! May I call you that?"

"I don't care."

She coughed again, and that cough seemed in some way to touch his heartstrings.

He bent over her and took one of the pale, claw-like hands.

"Rosa, what ails you? Aren't you well?"

"My throat aches something dreadful," she said with a little sob.

Johnny held her hand tightly, all the compassion and the sense of protection that Anna had never inspired rising inside him.

One of Anna's remedies occurred to him now. Michael had

caught a cold in his throat three weeks ago.

"Rosa," he said, "is there anything I could put round your neck?"

A vague question came into her eyes; then they became dull and hopeless again.

"Take something off the table," she murmured; "anything will do."

He approached the litter of garments and tore off a strip of white calico that was hanging from a petticoat. There was a glass of water on the chair beside the chop, and he poured it over the calico. Then he came back to the bed and wrapped the wet bandage round her neck.

For a second the cold made her gasp. Then a relief, wonderful to see, dawned on her face. The feel of Johnny's delicate, gentle fingers manipulating the bandage was different to anything she had ever known.

"Oh, this is just lovely," she said. "How good you are! How did you know what would feel so nice?"

Johnny was pleased. For a long time he could feel her eyes studying his face.

It was a beautiful face, Rosa thought. She had never seen anything like the æsthetic features or the blue, sombre eyes.

"What is your name?" she ventured, moved at last to curiosity.

"Johnny Croghan."

"Oh! You are very good."

"Well now," said Johnny, "won't you be telling me about yourself? How long are you in this house?"

She considered a moment.

"Near ten years it must be. Neil and I bought it when I married him. It was me named it 'The Star.' Don't you think that's a pretty name?" A flicker of pride crossed her face. "And it was me put up the flower paper in the big room. Maybe you'd not notice it now, the way it's got dirty and falling off. Oh, we made this house very grand and fine one time."

Johnny did not ask her what came afterwards. The pride of that long ago recollection had died off her face. She did not even look very sad.

The years had ground her down to a colourless, indifferent little waif, capable only of resignation.

But Johnny's presence—his sympathy—seemed to awaken something in her that had been nearly stamped out.

She gazed round the filthy, disordered room, and her cheeks began to burn.

"If I'd known you were really coming," she faltered. "I—I'd have put some of them things away and cleaned up a bit—"

Suddenly she put her head down and began to sob. Johnny could not bear this. He lifted her in his arms and held her close, stroking her unkempt hair.

"There, there!" he crooned over and over again. "There, there!" The feel of her clinging to him brought him a marvellous satisfaction and delight.

Chapter XXIII

Next morning Johnny lay in bed late, while Anna brushed her hair vigorously and pinned it at the back of her head.

"Mother, make yourself pretty again," cried Michael. "Daddy, last night mother did her hair—"

"Be quiet," Anna whispered sharply, and her cheeks grew hot. "Mother only dressed up that silly way to please you. You mustn't tell daddy about it."

She was really very much ashamed of herself, and glad that no one had seen her foolishness except the child. But she watched Johnny for the next few days, and really he seemed to be happier.

He spent long hours dreaming in the shop. All sorts of stray scenes and figures passed through his mind.

Rosa's tiny hands and her long, long eyelashes; a girl with a brown sunbonnet, leaning over a gate. Tim Derrybawn with the rope round his neck and the white light of innocence on his face. Yes, Johnny was happier. He was not tormented by the nightmare of Father Gilligan, and the terrible fears and dreams did not haunt him so often. For—and this is a curious thing—his mind had dwelt so much on the resigning of his post as executioner that he had come to believe he had actually resigned it. But he had not, and Anna knew it, though she thought only that Johnny had changed his mind.

Johnny kept as much as possible out of his wife's way. Her vigorous, efficient movements and her sharp voice nearly drove him mad with irritation. When she went out, he would creep upstairs to Michael, and they would feel like momentarily escaped prisoners and enjoy themselves thoroughly. Once she was out for hours, shopping, and they did not hear her come in.

She always hurried home, for she never knew what might happen when Johnny alone was in charge. She ran upstairs and opened the door.

A roaring fire met her eyes—Johnny had piled on all the coal that was to do for to-morrow.

He was lying now on the floor, his arms behind his head, and Michael was eating something out of a blue paper bag.

"We're after having games in the firelight," Johnny explained, looking up at her.

Anna snatched the bag out of the child's hand. "Will you look at this! The good sugar I bought only yesterday. There's not enough left for the tea to-night."

She slapped Michael soundly and he burst into tears.

"You're too hard on him," said Johnny.

"Too hard! Oh, you're a fool, Johnny. Whatever possessed you to give him the new sugar? But sure everything goes wrong in the house when I'm not in it. The Almighty certainly knew what He was doing when He put more women than men into this world."

Johnny walked sullenly down to the shop.

Anna had forgotten the incident by next day, but she did not know that each word remained in Johnny's mind, increasing the hatred and mutiny that was slowly growing within him.

But Father Gilligan did not leave the cobbler's shop alone very long.

One morning he came in and stood leaning on the counter. He seemed to have grown more gaunt and pale. There was a light behind his face that might break through at any moment and burn up his frail body.

"Johnny," he said, "do you remember I once talked of a penance that the Lord would exact from you in addition to your resignation?"

"A penance?" faltered Johnny, all his terror rushing back.

"Surely, you feel you must make some sacrifice for the wrong you have done to the world?"

Johnny was silent.

"Do the spirits of the men you hanged ever leave you in peace?" thundered the priest. "Tim Derrybawn, who was innocent—"

Johnny gave a cry of agony.

"What must I do?" he whispered, clutching at the priest's robe.

"You must leave this place and come with me into the world to preach God's message."

He started back.

"Leave Anna, your reverence, and my child?"

"That woman is all of the flesh and worldly. You must give them both up. Why, you have told me she cares nothing for you. What can she mean to you?"

Johnny twisted his hands together and fixed troubled eyes on the ground.

"Together we will walk the streets and the fields," chanted Father Gilligan. "The people shall listen to us, and the command of God shall take root in the earth."

Johnny sunk his face on his hands. Then the prophetic fire died out of the priest's eyes, and something that was almost sane took its place.

"Perhaps it is hard," he said quite gently, "yet when the Word came to me, I made the sacrifice."

Johnny had never seen him like this before. He flung down his tools and listened eagerly and rather wistfully.

"After I left the prison," went on Father Gilligan, "I went to live with my mother. When the Lord told me to bring His message to mankind, I spoke of it to her.

"She is like the woman upstairs; she could not understand. She begged me not to go, but the Lord strengthened me and I put her from me. That night she locked my door, but an angel told me what to do. So I let myself down from the window and fled away into the night."

There was a short silence.

Then the priest said in a lower voice:

"And now my work grows heavy on me. I want a disciple to carry on the message when I am gone. Will you come with me, Johnny Cregan?"

Johnny lifted his haggard face.

"Father, I can't tell you. Will you let me think? Will you let me wait a little longer?"

"I will give you thirty days. Come to my house by the river when you decide. I will pray for you to be helped to do the right."

He went away and the cobbler's shop did not see him again for many days.

But that decision haunted Johnny. It was scarcely ever out of his mind, and it became a terrible, unceasing nightmare.

Chapter XXIV

The next time Johnny climbed the steps and visited the squalid little room at the top he found it tidier and not quite so dirty.

The cracked mirror had been hung on a nail in the wall, and Rosa was standing in front of it, pinning up one side of her hair very carefully.

"Is that yourself, Johnny?" she cried, as he came in.

She turned joyfully towards him. "When I put out the rag an hour since, I was hoping and hoping to myself you'd be coming. Thank God you did."

She was a little flushed, and the colour was wonderfully improving to her face.

"What's up with you, Rosa?" said Johnny. "Is there anything the matter?"

"There is not. It's only the gladness in me at seeing you."

Johnny was touched. But he was also rather flattered. He did not think anyone had ever been glad to see him before.

He took her into his arms and her body seemed to give a great throb in response. As he released her she put her hand to her head.

"Look at the way my hair is falling—drat it! I'm after doing it up so nice for you. Would nothing do it but to be sliding out from the hairpins, making me look a holy show?"

He saw a hint of tears in her eyes.

"Don't be fretting about that now," he urged. "Sure, I like it down the same as up, so I do. It's pretty hair."

"I do be working so hard," said Rosa wearily, "most times I've not the time to be perking and peeping at myself in the glass. My hair had a curl to it when I lived with my mother in the County Clare."

Again the protective pity caught hold of Johnny.

"Have you to work hard, Rosa? What kind of work is it?"

"Sure it's only to be washing the plates and the glasses and cooking the bit of dinner and supper and giving a wipe over to the tables in the rooms below. But it seems like I can't do it. It doesn't matter how hard I go for them all, there's always more things to come after. I've a pain in my side sometimes that would make you weep."

Johnny kissed her again. He had a vague feeling that his kisses helped her and conveyed his pity. He liked to put his arms round her and kiss her; it seemed to satisfy something hungry and yearning inside him.

But she did not always complain. Once, indeed, she rose up rather hotly in defence of Neil.

"It's a dirty beast of a man your husband is," Johnny had said, after listening to her account of an ordinary day in her life. "I'd like to get my fist on his face one day soon. Maybe I will, too."

"Don't be saying the like of that, now," flashed Rosa, colouring. "He used to be a fine man once, and it's a strong, handsome man he is yet, so he is."

Johnny said nothing to this, but he thought over the words in the shop next morning. They had told him a great deal.

He loved stealing out in the evenings and climbing the old iron stairs up to the green door.

The atmosphere of Rosa's room was very soothing to him.

"I'm sorry the things aren't cleared away nice," she said timidly one night when he came in and found the room in worse disorder than he had ever seen it. "I hadn't the time to-day. I don't know how the things get like this."

"You needn't fret," said Johnny. "This is the way I like it. I never met the man who liked a room without a speck of dirt in it. It's good to be able to leave your things round where you want them, and come in with the mud on your feet, without someone fussing and scolding as if it was something terrible you were doing. I like coming here, Rosa."

So, as Rosa was a little slut herself, she let the dirt and disorder have their own way, and they were both completely happy.

When Johnny was with her, Anna and Michael seemed to him quite far away, like a sore memory.

Even the torturing alternative that Father Gilligan had put before him faded out of his mind.

Rosa's arms round him, and her response to his caresses, filled a blank in his soul.

So he was with her almost every evening. Sometimes he wondered curiously why Anna asked no questions.

But Anna, you see, never suspected. Her faith in Johnny was absolute. It never occurred to her to doubt him for a single moment.

She was always a little annoyed and angry when he went out in the evenings, but she never thought he had gone anywhere but to Father Gilligan's. And she did not mind that so much now.

The priest's influence did not seem to have such a depressing, terrifying effect on Johnny, who, she noted with satisfaction, seemed happier.

When he looked at her nowadays the old admiration was no

longer in his eyes. There was only a sombre, burning resentment. But she did not notice this, and if he never tried now to caress her or put his arms around her as he used to, she only thought he had grown out of the childishness and acquired more sense.

"He understands now what waste of time that sort of thing is," she, said to herself. "I always knew he would. I hate 'philandering.' There's no sense or meaning in it at all."

But her love for him had never wavered since the moment she had first confessed it to him, and it would never waver, whatever else might happen in the world.

Chapter XXV

To Rosa, of course, Johnny had come to be everything on earth. She lived mechanically through the day, with all its pain and weariness, longing, longing for the evening. She would put out her little signal with trembling hands, and then listen eagerly; listen and watch.

When she heard his step on the staircase she would feel little thrills all over her body. To lie in his arms was heaven. His beauty was a delight to her, and she felt—poor little starved slut—that he was good.

On the days that she could not put out the signal, she drooped and looked more sickly and feeble than ever. Johnny was the magnet that kept her attached to the earth.

"I don't know why Neil is so jealous," she said to him once, when she had not been able to see him for three days. "He does be watching me, watching me all the time. Well, one time I used to be breaking my heart with the jealousy when he—" she paused and a slight colour came into her face. "But that's done with now," she said. "I don't mind what he does anymore."

"When did you stop—caring?" Johnny asked.

"When I think of it now it seems that when the baby was born—"

"You had a baby?" cried Johnny.

"Ah, it died on us, the little creature, and it never baptised or blessed by a priest. I cried then to think it would never see God. After that I don't think I cared about anything anymore. Neil gave me this room then."

Johnny stroked her hair with his long slender fingers. "Poor wee girl! I wish I could take you away out of this."

"You couldn't," she said. "Neil would have the life of you."

"I'm not afraid of him."

She took his face in her hands and gazed at it for a long time.

"You're so brave," she said reverently at last. "What is there in the world now you'd be afraid of?"

"There's one thing," said Johnny in a low voice.

"What's that?"

"Oh! I'd be feared to death to be hanged. If I think of it at night, I scream. Waiting in the cell all night, and led out in the morning to die, the same as a dumb beast. Oh! I wouldn't mind how much they hurt me if so be they wouldn't do that to me."

Rosa took her hands from his face, and stood up in front of him.

"I'd be hanged if it ever could save you," she spoke very slowly. "Do you know I'd die for you, Johnny?"

He smiled and pulled her forward to kiss her.

He thought he loved her very much, but she knew better. She knew he did not love her at all. But she had learnt that men were never different, and she rejoiced in Johnny while she could, giving herself wholly up to him. If he had left her suddenly, she would never have blamed or reproached him for it. It would have conformed to the opinion which men had given her of themselves. But in spite of this she did her best to make herself attractive for him. They were pathetic, these crazy attempts. She would brush her hair into a fluffy fuzz over her forehead, heedless of the knotted tangles which showed at the back of her head, and the shapeless, protruding hairpins. She would scrub her face and throat with kitchen soap, and as she only looked at the front of herself in the mirror, she never thought of the smears on the back of her neck.

She would pull the torn heels of her stockings down into her shoes, and she tried to keep her hands over the dirty places in her apron when Johnny was there.

One day she crept timidly into a shop and bought a box of pink powder and a bottle of scent for sixpence. She had never thought of doing such a thing before, and she felt very daring.

She was coming towards the staircase on the back wall of "The Star" with the parcel hugged in her arms, when she met Neil.

She had not seen him near the steps for a long time, and the sight of him vaguely alarmed her.

"Where have you been?" he said.

"I'm after doing a bit of shopping, Neil."

"Let's see what you have there." He snatched the parcel from her and began to tear off the paper.

"Give that back, Neil," she cried. Goaded to fury, she sprang at him like a small wild thing.

He was so amazed at her passion that he let the parcel fall out of his hands. There was a tinkle of broken glass, and the green scent crawled sluggishly from under the paper.

"Is this what you were buying?" roared Neil Fogarty. "By the Hokey, if you ever dare put this filth on you, I'll scrape the guts out of you. I won't have my wife looking like a kept woman. D'you hear?"

For a moment she clenched her hands. Then all the passion passed from her face, and she took on her familiar worn, faded look.

"What did you buy them things for?" bullied Neil Fogarty. "You never done such a thing yet."

"I thought maybe they—they'd cover up these spots." She put her hand to her forehead where there were scarlet eruptions of disease and bad nourishment.

"You fool! If those don't come from eating too much!"

She laughed at that; a short, scornful laugh.

Then she began to mount the steps, and, after a hesitation, the man followed her.

The room at the top was still horribly dirty and unwholesome, though she had done a little lately to make it more fit for a human being to live in.

As Neil Fogarty glanced around, something like real disgust showed in his face.

"You filthy little vermin," he said. "If this room poisoned you, there'd be no wonder in it at all."

The woman made no answer. She went to the window and took in a bit of rag that was fixed to the sill.

"What's that?" barked Neil Fogarty, with quick suspicion.

"'Tis a bandage for my finger. I'm after washing it and putting it out to dry." She wrapped it hastily round her forefinger lest he should see how dirty it was.

He sat down on the one chair, and she fidgeted desperately about the room.

"I thought you were going out," she burst forth presently.

"I am not then. I changed my mind. Shall we have a cosy evening here instead?"

She backed away from him, pale with fright.

"No, no, Neil! Not that!"

"Arrah, stop your play-acting, woman! What's the matter with you at all?"

Then she came up to him, her pallid mouth trembling.

"Neil, do please go. I have the room to put tidy."

"Is it driving your husband away you are? No, Rosa, you look tired. Wouldn't you get cosy now, in the bed, if so be there's any comfort in the like of it."

He sat regarding her with his eyes half closed, and Rosa drew away from him again.

"Don't, Neil!" she whimpered. "I can't stand it."

"Why, this sort of thing is new. Not so long ago, there'd not be a word out of you."

"And you know well the reason why, too," she said miserably.

"Tell me."

"Because I thought you meant it." She began to cry. "Oh, the cruelty of you, the cruelty of you! I was happy enough with my mother."

"You came happily enough with me then," he said. "When did you start all these fine feelings?"

"After the child died on us," sobbed Rosa. "You were so cruel to me then, I knew I couldn't love you anymore."

"It was an ugly brat. Made me turn over to look at it. Ah! it's nonsense we're talking." He got up and advanced towards her with a silky, expectant tread.

"No more fooling, my dear. It's your turn to-night."

Rosa backed against the wall, but through her tears, her eyes shone with a strange, brave light.

"Go away from me, Neil Fogarty," she said.

He advanced smiling.

"If you dare try anything on, you'll be sorry," said Rosa, firmly and slowly.

He actually took a step backwards in his amazement.

"You're mad, Rosa! I never heard the like of that from you since I saw you first."

"Oh, I'm not afraid of you!" cried the woman hysterically, and two scarlet patches showed in her cheeks. "I don't care if you thrash the life out of me, I will say it."

"You've the drink taken surely. How dare you speak to me like that?"

He moved threateningly towards her, but she gave a shrill, reckless laugh.

"Ten years I've put up with you. How much longer did you think I was going on? If you lay one finger on me to-night, I'll—"

"You'll what?" he whispered, almost cowed by her hysterical fury.

Rosa's voice rose to a shriek.

"I'll kill you!"

The shriek was so loud that it penetrated through the whole house, and everyone in the tap-room and the card-rooms heard the words.

Chapter XXVI

It was a cold, stormy night.

Johnny, making his way up the street of the Three Marys, pulled up the collar of his coat as a protection against the driving rain.

Before he went out, Anna had come down to the shop.

"Will you be going out to-night?" she had asked.

"I will, so."

"Oh, Johnny, look at the pouring rain and the wind. You'll be soaked through, and you with a cold already. Come upstairs where I have a good fire and a bit of bacon for you."

"Woman, leave me be," he said angrily. "Will you be always running after me the same as if I was a child of two years and not a grown man?" And still there was not a suspicion in Anna's mind. She believed in Johnny's love as firmly as she thought he believed in hers.

Johnny turned off the street of the Three Marys and came at last to the quiet road where the back of "The Star" looked out.

The darkness was almost solid, and there were no lamps, but he found his way to the steps without hesitation.

Then, grasping the iron rail, he stood and listened. He always waited until the street was quite empty before he started to climb up.

The wind rose to a shrill howl, and blotted out all sound of footsteps. Except for that, the whole place was silent and deserted. There was not even a light in the kitchen windows.

Johnny started to mount the staircase; he knew quite well now where the broken steps were. He reached the green door and knocked.

"Come in," cried Rosa's tired little voice.

He opened the door and shut it quickly behind him lest a gust of wind should blow the candle out. Rosa was lying fully dressed on the bed, with a shawl wrapped round her, and her little, pale face pressed against it.

"I feel bad to-night," she said, trying to smile. "I was praying you'd come."

Johnny sat on the bed and slipped his arm under her shoulders raising her a little.

"Does that feel better, darling?"

"That's nice. Do you know, I like the way you do be knocking at the door waiting for me to call you in, instead of walking right in the way some would."

"Oh, I wouldn't think of walking right in on you," said Johnny, flushing.

"I know, you're different. I love you for that."

Johnny drew her close to him, and then something happened. There was a door at the other end of the room which opened on the stairs leading down to the tap-room. Someone was coming up those stairs very slowly and heavily.

"There's nothing on this landing only my room," whispered Rosa.

They sat together, listening, listening.

Then Rosa pulled herself out of his arms.

"You must get out of this, Johnny. Run out of the other door, now, while there's time." She pushed him with her puny hands.

"You fool! It's Neil, it's Neil."

But he would not move.

"Do you think I'm going to run away and leave you to face it?" he whispered fiercely.

A gust of wind skirled round the house, shrieking like a mad thing, and at the same moment the door at the other end of the room opened, and Neil Fogarty stood facing them.

The draught from the open door blew out Rosa's candle, but Neil Fogarty held another in his hand, the grease dripping on to his thick, clenched fingers. His face was very red, and he reeled a little against the wall.

"I thought so," he said unsteadily. "My God, if I'd known it before this I'd have thrashed the damned, miserable little life out of you."

Rosa shrank closer to Johnny, hiding her face in his rough coat.

"That's it," said Neil Fogarty, "ask him to protect you. The whining, milkfaced son of a—, I could knock the soul out of him with one hand."

"He's drunk," whispered Rosa, but she could feel Johnny's arm tense and hardened.

Then Neil Fogarty bent close to Rosa and mouthed the same horrible words he had said to her in the tap-room that first evening. Johnny flung off Rosa's arm and leaped to his feet.

"So you would, would you?" snarled Neil Fogarty, groping in his pocket for something.

There was murder in his eyes.

As his hand came out of his pocket, Johnny seized the thing that was in it, and fired close to the man's head.

Over Neil Fogarty's face there came a slow look of surprise, then—blankness.

He swayed once or twice before he fell with a terrific crash to the ground, dashing out the candle that he still held in his hand.

"Thank God," said Johnny.

Rosa clung, trembling, to him in the darkness. Downstairs they could hear a vague commotion. "You must go, you must go," she cried. "Maybe the police will be in on us after hearing that shot."

"I'm not afraid," said Johnny recklessly. "He deserved it and more—the brute!"

"Oh, don't be a fool, Johnny. You'll be caught. I'll see the police. If you go quick down the steps outside, they'll not think of you at all."

She pushed him to the door, as if galvanised into a new energy.

"Give me the pistol," she said, taking it from him.

Johnny turned to look back into the room.

They could hear a sound like water dripping on the floor.

"Do you think—is he dead?" he asked in a whisper.

"I don't know. Oh, I don't think so. Go on quick, now, before someone comes in."

She opened the door, and the wind blew the shawl off her shoulders. The moon came through the clouds for an instant, and he saw her face curiously strong and transfigured in the silver light.

"I want to kiss you, Johnny, once," she cried. She flung her arms round his neck and put three kisses on his forehead.

Then she half closed the door and pushed him out into the storm.

Chapter XXVII

When Anna woke up in the morning, she saw that Johnny was not in bed.

He must have got up early, she thought, as she put on her clothes. "It's not like him, but I believe he's trying to mend his reckless ways. I've often told him I hate to see him lying abed late in the mornings"—her face softened. "Poor Johnny, it's nice of him to try to please me. I'll praise him a little, when I go out, though I don't hold with praising."

But when she went into the outer room, she saw Johnny sprawling across a chair with his overcoat on, in a restless sleep.

She shook him angrily by the shoulder.

"Johnny, wake up, wake up."

He opened his eyes slowly and questioningly.

"What's the meaning of this," cried Anna.

For an instant his eyes were vacant and puzzled. Then he tried pettishly to writhe himself away from her.

"Let go of my shoulder, Anna, it's a rough hand you have."

"Was it here you were all night, instead of coming to your bed like a decent Christian?" she scolded, for she detested irregularity.

"It was not, then, but walking the streets. Last night I felt I couldn't sleep. At three o'clock I come in, and I must have gone asleep here before I knew it."

All of which was perfect truth. But his reckless exhilaration had passed away, and he was feeling rather cold and anxious.

"I sleep so sound I never knew you hadn't come to bed," said Anna. "You stay out so late these times, Johnny, and you never used to. I wish you wouldn't."

"Why not?" said Johnny. He flashed a glance at her and saw that she looked faintly worried.

"There's no knowing what might happen to you in the streets at night. You say yourself there's folks that bear you a grudge"—but she was really thinking of the priest.

"Will you have sense?" said Johnny, greatly relieved. "Is it a child or an idiot I am, the way you do be fussing and prying after me—fussing and prying?"

"You're in a bad humour to-day," she laughed. "Will you come to your breakfast, now, while I get the child dressed?"

Johnny had not been in the shop more than an hour that morning when Mrs. Carey rushed in, her hair falling and her face red with excitement.

"Where's herself, Johnny? Will you call her down, for there's great news to tell."

"What is it at all?" said Johnny, lifting his eyes from his work.

"Call her quickly now, for there's others will be coming in to tell it here, and the Lord have mercy on me if I'm not the first." Her voice rose shrilly, "Mrs. Croghan, Mrs. Croghan, ma'am."

"I can't come, I'm doing the floor," called Anna.

"I won't be letting you miss the news, ma'am. I'll come up the stairs to you."

She started to mount the stairs, but Anna appeared in the doorway above and came down to the shop, her hands still wet and soapy.

"Paddy Clancy's shouting it through the streets, and he after having it straight from Fogarty's pub," said Mrs. Carey. "It's a wonder you didn't hear him."

"What is it?" asked Anna, moved at last to curiosity. Johnny bent his head very low over his stitching.

"There were terrible doings at 'The Star' last night," began Mrs. Carey in a sepulchral tone, but delighted with the impression she had made. "They're saying Neil Fogarty was found dead in the wee room at the top of the house at half-past twelve of the clock."

She paused dramatically for effect.

"Are you mad, Mrs. Carey?" cried Anna. "What's this you're saying?"

"With a pistol it was done," the other woman described in a hoarse whisper. "They were all in the bar when Neil says he has business somewhere, and away with him out of the room. And if you'll believe me, ma'am, not ten minutes after, a shot was heard upstairs.

"Well then nothing would do the police—bad cess to them—that do be watching Neil Fogarty's pub night and day sometimes—the interfering villains—but to be rushing in to see what was happening. Most of them that were in the bar took to their heels, the way the police wouldn't be concerning them in it at all. But Paddy Clancy and a few gossoons who fear neither God nor the devil, followed the police over the house searching and prying into every room."

The relish with which Mrs. Carey told the story proclaimed a deep regret that she had not been there to explore by torchlight all those bare, sinister rooms.

"Well, they come to a wee room at the top," she proceeded, "and what did they find there but Neil lying dead on the floor with his ear all torn by reason of the bullet that had passed through his head, and the whole place saturated with blood."

She paused again, but this time she was satisfied with Mrs. Croghan's amazement and excitement.

"Good gracious," cried Anna, "how in heaven's name did it happen?"

"But there's more to come," broke in the other woman, her words falling over each other in their haste to be out of her mouth. "They found Rosa in the wee room, too, and she in the act of throwing something out of the window. But they caught her before she had time, and what do you think it was, ma'am—a pistol! Well, Paddy Clancy wasn't let stay while they were talking to Rosa, and someone dragged him down the stairs the way he wouldn't be listening at the keyhole and he outside of the door. That was a great pity."

"But what happened?" said Anna, breathlessly. "What did they do with her?"

Mrs. Carey had reached her climax.

She spoke very slowly and effectively.

"The police—themselves and their high falutin' talk—are after arresting Rosa, on what they call circumstantial evidence, for the murder of her husband."

Chapter XXVIII

When the two women left Johnny, alone in the shop, a hot, fierce anger surged over him.

Strange to say the anger was against Rosa, and yet not so strange, for she had never meant more to him than the transient delight of a bar of chocolate, and she had known it, though he had not, then.

"The fool, the fool!" he muttered to himself. "Why couldn't she have hid the pistol before they came up? Sure they're all like that. You can't trust women. Why was she in the room along with the man at all? Och, it's a poor simple thing she is with no brains at all, for all her high talk about getting away from the police. She'll have to tell now to get herself out of this trouble."

As this thought took shape, he felt the first inkling of a dreadful, unspeakable fear. It was only the beginning, so it was quite faint then, but it grew day by day, and lay down with him at night, and he never got away from it.

It was worst in the shop, where it was very dark and every customer that came in might be a policeman. He would sit very still sometimes and listen for the regulation steps outside his door.

Flip! Flop! Flip! Flop!

That was only Carl Vanelli with his barrow of old clothes. His boots were always too large for him.

"It's just a matter of time," Johnny would whisper, with his head held in his hands. "A matter of time till Rosa tells everything and they come for me."

He never thought of confiding in Anna. A sort of inherited fatalism or, perhaps, just torpor made him unable to do anything definite. He just suffered while the days passed and passed and nothing happened.

Anna, too, was worried.

For one thing the shop was no longer paying. They had never had many customers owing to the fact that most of the inhabitants of St. Brigid Street went barefoot, but it had brought in just enough money for their food. Anna hated breaking into the hoard in the dresser, except for necessities such as Johnny's overcoat and decent clothes for them all. These necessities, by the way, gave her a certain prestige among the women, whose husbands went coatless, and whose children were almost naked. But lately Johnny had not even pretended to work. He sat motionless and brooding behind the counter, and when she rebuked him sharply for his laziness, he turned on her with hot, angry words.

"He's not well," she thought. "Goodness knows what's ailing him. I suppose I ought to take him to the doctor."

The only reason that she did not take him was the queer prejudice of her class against doctors and dentists and everything except natural remedies.

And sometimes of course he behaved quite normally as if nothing was wrong with him at all.

What really worried her, though, was the fact that lately she had had to take money from the drawer in the dresser for food as well as other things.

"It's such a pity when we'd got nearly enough for the grocer's shop," she regretted. "I do wish Johnny would pick up and get to work again."

If she had not thought Johnny was ill, she would have been very angry indeed with him.

She was intensely interested in the case of Rosa Fogarty, partly because, though she had never actually spoken to her, she had heard a great deal about her and had been sorry for her warped, spoiled life.

But it was when she spoke of Rosa that Johnny behaved "his queerest."

"You know they've made a mistake—those fools of police," she said once to him. "Rosa couldn't have done it. A little underfed creature like that. I know it's a mistake."

"Yes, it's a mistake," said Johnny.

"It won't be long before her trial. Never believe me again, if they don't find out the person that did it—man or woman—then."

"Oh, they'll find him out," said Johnny.

He shuddered and covered his face with his hands.

"Then God help us all," he muttered.

One day, because she was a humane woman, and suffering many tribulations herself just now, Anna went to visit Rosa Fogarty at Portobello Prison.

She had never been in a prison before, but she was not the woman to be depressed by its atmosphere and its grey stone walls.

When she saw Rosa she realised that the little woman had changed.

Her hair was neatly arranged, and there was a peaceful look on her white, pinched face.

"Good day, Mrs. Fogarty," said Anna. "I don't think you know me. I am Mrs. Croghan."

"Mrs. Croghan?" the query was abrupt and startled. "Mrs. *Johnny* Croghan?"

"Yes. My husband keeps a cobbler's shop in St. Brigid Street."

Rosa gave her a long, searching look.

"Why did you come?" she asked presently.

"I thought you'd like someone to come and see you and talk to you a bit. Of course I don't know you, but everyone is talking about this down our way"—she stopped awkwardly.

"Go on," said Rosa. "Tell me what they do be saying about me."

"Oh, come now, Mrs. Fogarty. Let's not talk too much about it. Tell me what's it like here. Are they very hard on you?"

Rosa closed her eyes rather wearily.

"No, 'tis very restful. There's more peace here than ever there was at home."

She had clasped her hands limply together, and, now that they were clean and white-nailed, their puny smallness aroused in Anna almost the same pity that they had in Johnny.

"But you're coming out soon," she said quickly. "Your trial's in a few days and, depend on it, those fools of police will be sorry they ever arrested you."

"They will not then," said Rosa composedly. "Why should they be?"

"What do you mean, Mrs. Fogarty?"

"Well, aren't I guilty? I did kill Neil that Tuesday night."

"What!" cried Anna. "You don't know what you're saying."

She stared again at the colourless, meagre little woman, and would not believe that she had ever clutched a pistol and shot the life out of a big man.

"It's the truth I'm telling you," said Rosa. "And I don't care who knows it."

There was truth in her voice, and Anna thought she ought to feel repulsed.

"Well, I suppose you had provocation," she said rather coldly, "and, of course, if you have a clever counsel, you may get off. But I wouldn't say these things if I were you, even to me."

"Is it get off? Sure, I don't want that at all. If they ask me about it, it's the truth I'll be telling them, like I told you."

Anna stared at her in amazement.

"You'll plead guilty? I don't understand."

"I did kill Neil," said Rosa obstinately, "and I'll tell no lies about it. There's a kind gentleman does be coming sometimes to talk to me, and he says if I don't tell the truth, he might make them think someone else did it and I'd get off, maybe."

"But that's what you want," cried Anna, still unable to believe.

"It is not then," a spasm contracted the pallid face. "It wouldn't do for them to be thinking that at all. They won't, will they?"

She lifted her eyes, with a sort of quivering appeal.

"But don't you know," said Anna, speaking very slowly, as if to a child, "that if they find you guilty, you will be hanged? Don't you understand that?"

Rosa lowered her eyes and began to pluck her dress nervously with her fingers.

"Oh, I know that," she said in a low voice. "I try not to think of it."

"I can't understand you," said Anna. She rose to her feet. "Mrs. Fogarty, won't you tell me why you're behaving like this?"

"I shot my husband," said Rosa stubbornly, "and I don't care who knows it, nor what happens to me, nor anything."

As Anna regarded the faded, curiously undefiant little figure before her, she felt again that she ought to be repulsed by it, but she was not.

"Aren't you sorry for it, now?" curiosity moved her to ask.

"I am not then. Maybe I'll tell that to the judge too."

They stood facing each other, Rosa with that odd, searching look again in her eyes.

Then Anna did a curious thing. The secret woman within her, who had done all the foolish, impulsive things in her life, like walking penniless to Dublin, and dressing up in an old white frock, again took command.

"You poor little thing," said Anna. "I don't know why, but I'm sorry for you. Somehow, I don't think you've ever been very happy," and she put her arms round Rosa Fogarty and kissed her.

Chapter XXIX

That evening Johnny did not go out. He had stayed at home much more during the last few days.

He sat instead by the fire, and Anna, looking up once from her sewing, caught such a hopelessly miserable look on his face that she was quite startled.

She tried to attract his attention.

"Do you know what I did to-day?" she said brightly. "I went to Portobello Prison and saw Mrs. Fogarty."

Instantly he started up, as if galvanised by electricity.

"You saw Rosa Fogarty?" he cried. His eyes had a peculiar, strained look.

"Oh what a fool I am," muttered Anna, losing her needle in her annoyance. "Couldn't I have remembered the Fogarty affair always makes him queer." Aloud she said, "Nothing much happened, Johnny, I only went because I felt sorry for the poor woman."

"What did she say? I must know, I must know!" he caught her arm fiercely, as if trying to shake the words out of her.

"Johnny, what's the matter with you? You look so queer."

He tried to control himself, and dropped back into his seat. "I only want to know. Aren't you going to tell me anything at all?"

"She's such a queer one," Anna said reflectively. "I can't really understand her. Johnny, if we could get the neighbours to sign a petition—"

"Will you tell me?" he cried hoarsely, "why aren't you telling me?"

She looked at him in surprise.

"You're very impatient. I didn't know you were so interested in the case. Well, she's going to plead guilty. She insists—she told me quite shamelessly—that she did shoot the man, Neil. It really is queer. But Johnny, the funny part is that somehow I don't feel she's telling the truth. I can't tell you how it is. I just felt it whilst she was talking. Of course, the court mayn't accept her plea, but if they do and she's found guilty, do you think we could all sign a petition for a reprieve—"

He interrupted her with a guttural cry, and sprang to his feet.

"Don't be talking anymore about it, for God's sake, it's vile!"

He strode out of the room, and the door crashed behind him.

"Well, now, I wonder what's the matter with him at all?" said Anna, but her face was troubled.

Johnny was rushing through the dark, filthy streets. He sank ankle-deep in snow and mud, but he never felt it.

Something drew him to the river. When he reached the quays, he stood and looked down at the turgid, sluggish water.

On the opposite bank, tall, old warehouses were faintly outlined in the darkness. All round him were heaps of refuse, and the sound of barges creaking at their moorings. No one else was in sight.

"What the devil does this mean?" he smote the wall with his clenched hand. "She's lost her memory in the fear of being arrested. She thinks it was she killed Neil Fogarty." There were misty lights moving on the opposite side. He stared at them without seeing them. "I can't let her hang," he whispered, "I can't let them hang her. It would he a terrible thing to do, and she an innocent woman. To the police I will he going to-morrow morning. But that may mean the rope for me. Mother of God, the rope! There was Job Moran, they hanged him, and him not able to sleep at night." He laid his cheek against the cold stone. "O God, O God, what will I do?"

But the stone gave him no guidance or comfort. He walked home, soaked with rain, his teeth chattering in the cold.

Anna was terribly anxious about him in the days that followed.

He would eat scarcely any food and he muttered and screamed sometimes in his sleep, turning and tossing so that she could get no rest.

"Your husband looks ill, Mrs. Croghan," said Mrs. Carey one day, "do you know what's wrong with him at all?"

Anna hated these interferences and kindly meant suggestions.

"I expect it's only a chill or a bit of indigestion," she said shortly.

"I wouldn't wonder. Why don't you put him to bed?"

"I did, yesterday."

"Well, now, isn't that the queer thing! Danny saw him on the quays that same day, and his head down on the wall like as if he was drunk—begging your pardon, ma'am."

Johnny had refused to stay in bed, and had flung himself out of the house when she insisted, but Mrs. Carey was not going to hear that.

"I let him get up after a bit," said Anna; "after all it's only some passing trouble. He'll be all right in a day or two."

If she could have seen Johnny walking ceaselessly up and down the quays fighting it out, fighting it out with his heart and courage almost broken!

He could not bear to stay in the shop. There were shadows there, and horrible things that lurked in the corner where the rope and pinioning-straps were.

He spent hours on the quays, striding up and down until his body ached and he had to throw himself down to rest.

But his tortured brain never slept.

At night he used to stare down into the water where the reflection of a street lamp was thrown in a million points of broken radiance, as if expecting Rosa's face to rise up through it and gaze at him with her weary, drab eyes.

Once, Anna made him stay at home for the evening.

Johnny felt too tired to resist her.

He sank on to his stool, and took his head in his hands to stop the hammering in it.

Michael was playing with his doll, humming under his breath as he always did. Presently his voice rose louder in the plaintive tune with its grotesque words that he had learnt from Johnny.

> *"And then I hanged my Annie*
> *(Away, boys, away!)*
> *I hanged her up so canny—"*

Anna turned to interrupt the song she hated, but Johnny was before her.

"Will you stop that, you little devil! Am I to stay here to be tormented and driven mad? God, let me get out of this."

But he came back again, as he always did, tortured and miserable with the problem still unsolved, and a dreadful uncertainty hanging over him of what would happen in the end.

Chapter XXX

St. Brigid Street was keenly interested in the Fogarty affair.

This interest took its usual form.

Some were in sympathy with Rosa and some condemned her. There were a great many street rows and, consequently, the police kept their eyes on the district, including the street of the Three Marys.

At any hour of the day Anna, working upstairs would hear excited arguing voices. They were often women.

"Poor Rosa Fogarty! Hadn't she great pluck now to shoot down that dirty beast of a man, and he with never a moral or a bit of good in him, at all."

"Who are you to be talking of morals, Mrs. Doyle? Sure doesn't everyone know—"

"Hold your whisht, you! It's St. Vitus' Dance you have in your tongue."

"It would tear the heart out of you to be watching the poor girleen treated as if she was vermin, let alone a dog or a cat."

"Divil a bit of decency or pride she had in her then, the shameless thing! I seen her—"

"It's a great shame in you, Sarah Dillon, to be talking the like of that about a woman who'll be helping you up the steps to heaven and you stumbling and falling by reason of the sins on your soul."

"Let you wait till I get at you, Mrs. Carey, if I had my foot on the crooked face of you, it's not soon I'd be lifting it off again."

The stentorian voice of a policeman:

"Move on there, now! Don't be creating a tumult."

Anna was relieved to find that Johnny never wanted to join in these brawls.

To Johnny, indeed, they were a horror. He would wait cowering in the shop, while they fought and argued, and Rosa's name was flung from mouth to mouth. He did not dare to go out, lest they should read his secret on his face.

When the streets were silent, he dashed out of the shop and down to the quays where he could breathe and think more easily. He would lean over the wall, looking down into the river for hours and hours.

Once, he saw Rosa's face in the water, rising up to meet him, like a drowned face.

He threw stones at it to make it go away. Then he put his head down on his hands. "What will I do? What will I do? This is killing me."

One night he went to "The Wild Harp" and drank glass after glass of whisky. In a few hours he forgot everything. He said some queer, dangerous things, and one man in a green corduroy coat listened intently.

Johnny reeled home very late, and Anna was terribly alarmed when she saw his glazed eyes and his nose which was quite red.

She was angry too the next morning.

"I'm simply ashamed of you, Johnny, I never thought you'd go and do such a thing. It's too bad of you."

He resolved not to do it again.

The forgetfulness was good while it lasted, but the headache afterwards was terrible. It stayed for a long, long time.

Anna had grown accustomed to his staying out late in the evenings, and she always locked the door and went to bed early. Johnny had his own key.

One morning, he was sitting by the fire and Anna was preparing to go out for her marketing. She hung a large basket on her arm and unlocked the drawer in the dresser to take some money.

Then Johnny heard her give a startled cry. He looked up and saw her standing still, a horrified look on her face.

"What's up with you?" he asked indifferently.

"Johnny, the money's gone! It's stolen. Whatever can have happened?"

"Gone?" he echoed stupidly.

"It's not there. Come and see for yourself." She was searching wildly among the other things in the drawer. "Someone must have got in and taken it."

As yet, she could not quite take in the meaning of the loss. "Our money! Our money!" she kept repeating. "All our money gone!"

Suddenly, an accusation flashed into her eyes. She pointed at Johnny.

"I know what happened. You didn't lock the door last night."

He raised his eyes, and a slow, puzzled frown wrinkled his forehead.

"I remember now," he muttered. "Last night I lost the key when I was out. When I come to the door, I found I hadn't it in my pocket."

"Why didn't you take mine?"

"Och, I forgot about it when I come upstairs."

She stared at him, absolutely amazed at his carelessness and stupidity.

"Well, you've ruined us at last," she said, slowly.

Then the sense of her appalling loss swept over her, coupled with Johnny's sullen indifference as he stood regarding her, with his hands in his pockets.

She sat down at the table, and burst into tears. For five minutes she cried loudly and with absolute unrestraint.

Johnny watched her with passing curiosity. He had never seen Anna cry.

Then he walked out of the room.

"It's awful, it's awful!" sobbed Anna, giving way completely for the first time in her life. "And, oh, I wish Johnny could understand. I don't know what's the matter with him these days."

But her surrender did not last longer than five minutes. She sat up straight and scrubbed her eyes with her handkerchief; she was hotly ashamed of herself.

"I'm not going to be foolish," she said rather fiercely. "Let me see now what can be done."

Her force and determination came back to her, strengthening her against this overwhelming blow.

"I think we can manage all right," she was able to tell Johnny quite brightly in the evening. "You see, the shops will give us credit for a time, as we've always paid so regular. Johnny, couldn't you get to work again in the shop? That would bring us something."

"Work!" said Johnny. "It would drive me mad."

He turned away from her and brooded sullenly over the fire.

"Well, perhaps it would do you more good to rest a bit," she said. "We could maybe sell something—that dresser would fetch a price—until you're well enough to start with the shoes again. I hate buying on credit. Dear, dear, it's an awful thing to happen to us."

As she spoke, Johnny had a vision of the man in the corduroy coat leaning forward to listen to the things he said at "The Wild

Harp." But, in his own terrible distress, that memory could rouse no pangs of conscience.

"Will you stop lamenting after the money?" he said, with slow resentment. "A few pounds stolen from us! You have no knowledge at all of sorrow."

"Johnny, I don't believe you care a bit."

She was puzzled and a little hurt, and she was turning away when something bright protruding from his pocket caught her eyes. It was the top of the gaudy handkerchief she had bought for him at Christmas.

For some absolutely inexplicable reason the sight of it brought all her love and pity to the top. She went back to him and put her arm round his shoulders. It was the first spontaneous caress she had ever given him, and it was rather shy and awkward.

"Johnny, I'm very worried about you," she said gently. "Won't you tell me what's wrong?"

"There's nothing wrong"—he jerked her arm off his shoulder.

Scarcely aware of the repulse, she knelt down by his side.

"I know you're in trouble. Well, then, you're ill. I'm sure I could help you, Johneen, if you'd tell me."

"You? Ah, leave talking nonsense. There's nothing the matter with me."

With a little sigh, she got up from her knees and stood looking down on his bent head.

"My God, I wish we had moved out of this when we had the money," he said suddenly.

"I wish we had too. We only needed a few more pounds to buy the big shop. But it's no good going over that now."

His head sunk lower and lower.

"And I suppose it would have happened just the same," he murmured, too softly for her to hear.

On the day of Rosa's trial there was wild excitement in St. Brigid Street.

"You're coming, Mrs. Croghan?" called Mrs. Carey as she passed the cobbler's shop in the middle of an eager, ragged crowd.

Anna leaned out of the window.

"I'm not coming, Mrs. Carey. I must take care of Johnny, and I won't let him go."

"Maybe you're right. He's not himself at all these days."

The procession was moving on.

"Drop in when you come back and tell me how the case goes," called Anna.

"I'll do that, Mrs. Croghan. It will be a queer case, I'm thinking."

Johnny never knew how he lived through that day. His blood and his head were on fire. He spent most of the time walking up and down on the quays, walking up and down, gnawing his fingers, because he could not keep still. When he stopped walking, his heart beat like a hammer and hurt him.

His legs felt as weak as jelly, and once they gave way under him and he fell, bruising himself on the stones.

He tried to pray: "Oh, God, let her be found not guilty," but he always quickly revoked the prayer. The suspense nearly killed him.

In the evening, when he judged the trial to be over, he went back to the shop, running all the way, heedless of people and traffic.

"Is Mrs. Carey back?" he asked Anna breathlessly.

"Johnny, how awful you look. You shouldn't have run like that. Your heart is beating terribly."

"Is Mrs. Carey back?" he screamed.

"No, she's not home yet. Johnny, do come and lie down, you

look so ill."

He flung himself on the bed, but the moment he lay still the terror and suspense made him feel faint. He got up and paced the room up and down.

Five steps this way, five steps that way. Would Mrs. Carey never come?

There were steps below in the shop. Anna opened the bedroom door.

"Johnny, she's here now. Will you come and hear all about it?"

To her surprise he cowered back against the wall.

"No, no," he whispered.

In her own anxiety to learn what had happened at the trial, his behaviour did not strike her as odd.

She hurried downstairs.

Johnny covered his face with his hands. It had been absolutely beyond him to go to the court, and now it was absolutely beyond him to go down and hear the verdict from Mrs. Carey.

"I can't, I can't!" he moaned. "God give me strength."

And strength was given to him.

In a few minutes he felt able to walk downstairs to the shop, though he had to cling tight to the banisters.

There had been the usual arguing and prevarication on the parts of the witnesses, which by reason of their untaught mentalities had been fairly easily unravelled by astute cross-examination.

"There was a great crowd in the court," Mrs. Carey was saying as Johnny came in. "Rosa Fogarty looked better than I've seen her these eight years past. But it was a mighty queer way she went on. She wouldn't help her counsel at all. Everything he said she gave the lie to the next minute. He was in a mighty rage, I can tell you, poor man. You see, it went hard with them to accept her guilty plea."

She stopped for breath.

"What happened?" Johnny said in a strangled voice.

"Well, you see, some of the witnesses, it came out, had heard her say to Neil, the night before the murder, 'I'll kill you.' Shouted it, she did, at the top of her voice. When they asked her, Rosa says, says she, 'I said that. And I meant it,' says she, as cool as you please. So, you see, the case was against her from the first. The jury weren't out above twenty minutes."

She paused again. There was a terrible, strained tension in the air. Johnny was breathing in hard gasps.

"The verdict?" whispered Anna. "The verdict?"

"Oh," said Mrs. Carey slowly. "Rosa Fogarty got what she seemed to want, and what she deserved—the shameless hussy. She got herself condemned to death."

Chapter XXXI

Anna was bending over Johnny as he lay in bed. How ill and tired he looked, with all the lines of fear and misery carved on his face as if they would never go away. His long eyelashes touched his cheeks, which were as white as the pillow. She passed her hand gently over his rough, curly hair. As she touched him, he opened his eyes and came to himself.

"What happened?" he said thickly.

"Oh, Johnny, thank goodness you've come round. I was beginning to get scared. Don't you remember, you fainted down in the shop when Mrs. Carey was telling us about the trial? She helped me carry you up here."

The dazed look passed from him and a horrid convulsion went over his face. He buried his head in the pillow.

"Don't you feel better?" asked Anna anxiously.

He gave a little moan.

"Oh, dear, I'm afraid you're going to be ill," she said.

He sat up at that, his fingers clutching the top of the blankets.

"I'll be all right," he muttered.

"Shall I stay here with you?"

"No, no! Go from me now, and I'll get better."

"Call me, if you want anything, Johnny," she said half wistfully, and closed the door on him.

A few hours later he came into the outer room, fully dressed.

"Oh, Johnny, you should have stayed in bed for one day at least," said Anna vexedly.

"I couldn't stay in bed. I had to get up. It kills me to stay still these days."

"You didn't used to be like that. You'd be sitting there over the fire doing nothing all day, if you had your way."

"I'm changed, Anna."

"You are indeed. I don't know what's the matter with you at all."

He fidgeted about the room.

"Don't keep on at me," he said irritably. "I'm well enough."

"Well, I'll let you stay up to-day. If I think you're ill to-morrow I'll hide all your clothes, the way you won't be able to get up."

He came and sat down by the fire.

Anna scrutinised him sharply over her work.

There was a hectic flush on his face which she interpreted as a sign of returning health.

"Well, it seems you are better," she said with relief, "and if you are, I'll tell you something I've thought of."

He did not answer, so she continued, her eyes bent on her sewing.

"Since that money was stolen on us—"

"What money?" said Johnny vacantly.

"Don't be silly. The money we had in the drawer there. Don't go wool-gathering, Johnny; I want you to listen."

He fixed his eyes on her face, and she began again.

"Of course, I thought before the money went, that if Rosa Fogarty was found guilty and condemned, you couldn't be expected to carry out the execution."

He made a sharp movement, but she continued without noticing. "You see, it's all changed now, and after all you only spoke once to her. They'll expect you to do the job, as they don't know anything about that. And it will bring us ten guineas, which will be something to start on."

She looked up and saw his eyes fixed on her with such utter horror that she blushed.

"Of course it sounds awful, Johnny. I'm sorry for the poor woman, and I wouldn't ask you if it wasn't for the money going from us like that. But now we can't afford to let ten guineas slip out of our hands."

She bent towards him, but he sprang away from her as though she were something horrible.

"My God!" he cried hoarsely, "how can you talk like that? Isn't there a bit of decency in you at all?"

"Come, Johnny, there's no need to make a fuss. If there was a chance of the poor woman being proved innocent after all, there'd be nobody gladder than myself. But I suppose the court must know, and she's rightly condemned, though I still can't help feeling she's not guilty. She must die, Johnny, and if you don't take the execution, someone else will and the ten guineas along with it."

"I'll not do it," he said.

"You'd understand if you weren't ill. Don't you realise, Johnny, we haven't a penny; we've no money at all! I don't know how we're going to manage. And we could hang on till we get the ten guineas, if you'd help us. I do think it selfish of you."

"I'll not do it," he cried in anguish. "Haven't I told you? Why are you tormenting me?"

She considered a moment. Then a light flashed across her mind.

"I've been wondering why you wouldn't. I know now. It's that priest, with his nonsense and his lies. Oh, Johnny, don't you realise he's just a maniac? Why will you listen to him at all? There's not a word of sense in his ravings and his goings on." She rose and laid her hand on his shoulder. "Just forget everything he's told you, Johnny, and do what I ask you. You wouldn't like to get us all into debt and disgrace, would you?"

"God help me against her!" he muttered, and hid his face in his hands.

After this came Johnny's first thoughts of suicide. He went in the evening to the quays and looked down at the black, slimy water gurgling against the wall. He could not swim. He had never been in the water before. Was it very deep here, and did it take a long time to kill you?

He picked up a stone and threw it in. It made a little splash and he could see it for a second, sinking under the water.

Sudden horror and revulsion seized him. He turned and ran away as if someone was pursuing him, bursting into the cobbler's shop with a grey shadow on his face.

"What's the matter?" cried Anna. "Come to the fire. You're frozen with the cold."

"Oh, Anna, it was me killed Neil Fogarty," he said.

"What's happened to you at all? Sit down there, while I make you a cup of tea. I was so worried about you."

"She doesn't believe me," he muttered, letting his head sink down on his knees. "The police wouldn't either, if I went and told them."

"What are you saying?" asked Anna, busy with the kettle.

"Nothing. Oh, I wish I was dead. I wish I could die to-night in my sleep."

It was the last thought he ever had of giving himself up to Justice.

Chapter XXXII

After this Johnny began to be tormented by pains in his head. They passed through his brain sharply and scorchingly, like flashes of lightning. He also began to find it hard to think clearly.

One day Anna saw him tie a broad leather strap round his temples.

"What on earth are you doing?" she asked in astonishment.

"Och, I'm trying to stop something inside my head breaking to pieces," he said.

"Well, of all the nonsense! I declare to goodness, Johnny, I wonder sometimes if you're all there."

"Let me be," he said savagely. "You never understand anything at all."

He still spent a certain amount of time in the shop, where Michael would hear him muttering to himself for hours.

Michael, at this time, had a queer, fascinated fear of his daddy. Sometimes, the fascination drew him into the shop, and Johnny would talk to him as he had in the old days.

"Before you hang a person, you have to test the rope with a bag of cement the same weight as the person. What weight, I wonder, would Rosa be? There would be a short drop for her. A little, little thing she was; you could hold her in one hand. Her hair was always falling down. It would make you laugh, so it would, to see the hairpins falling on to the floor out of her head."

Michael would laugh then, because his daddy did.

Johnny pulled the old, charred rope out of his pocket and put it round Michael's neck.

"It's a wee bit of rope would kill you. I couldn't get my head into that noose. It would fit Rosa. They never gave her enough to eat."

"I'll make a noose for daddy," cried Michael, twining the rope round Johnny's neck.

"Take that off this minute, you little devil," screamed Johnny. "The feel of it's dreadful. If you do that again, I'll have the life of you."

Michael, terrified, had run upstairs to his mother. He never told Anna any of the things Johnny said to him. There are some things a child cannot speak about.

But Johnny was not often in the shop. Perpetual motion was the only thing that assuaged the agony in his mind. He liked to walk in the evenings when there were fewer people about to stare at his furtive, miserable figure.

One evening, a few days before the date fixed for Rosa Fogarty's execution, he was wandering as usual by the river, when he felt a hand laid on his shoulder.

He turned, with a slight scream, and found himself looking into a gaunt, pale face.

"Father Gilligan!" he whispered.

"Your eyes are frightened," said the priest, studying him, "and your face looks as though you have passed through Purgatory. What has happened to you, Johnny Cregan?"

"Nothing," said Johnny, and he bent his head because he feared the priest could look into his soul through his eyes.

"Fool!" cried Father Gilligan. "God has sent you a warning."

"What are you saying, Father?"

"I see a great fear in your eyes. It is a warning of the curse which hangs over you like a thunder-cloud. You have desisted from your unholy work, but more is demanded of you. You must atone! You must atone!"

He raised his arms and face to the stars in a sort of ecstasy. Johnny watched him with all the old fascination this creature exerted over him.

"Have you your answer to the alternative I put before you a month ago?" said the priest.

"The alternative?" faltered Johnny.

"I must speak simply to you. I asked you to come with me out of this city and preach the message of God to the world. I gave you thirty days to consider, and the time has gone. What is your answer?"

Then Johnny looked up, and the light of a street lamp revealed a longing hope in his eyes.

"I'm thinking, maybe I will," he said slowly. "I want to get out of this place. It's killing me."

"Then my prayers have been answered. I have wanted you so much to be my companion, Johnny Cregan, in the hard path God has set before my feet. I will thank Him for He has given you light."

Again he lifted his face, and his lips moved passionately.

"Your wife? Your child?" he said to Johnny. "You have cast them aside at the command of your God?"

"Anna wouldn't care if I went from her. She never understands. She is nothing to me now. Maybe I could forget and start fresh if I went with you."

The priest's eyes burned in his head. He grasped Johnny's hand.

"Together we will preach the sin of capital punishment through this poor country which is yet beloved of God. She will be the first to see the light, and the world will follow her. We will gather more disciples, and the message of God will at last prevail!"

"When can we start?" said Johnny. "This is a terrible place for me. It's the country I want, and the flowers and the long roads. Maye I'll be all right then when I can forget."

"I'll leave the city in three days," said Father Gilligan. "On the morning of the third day, before the birds wake, come to me in my hut by the river-side, and we will start together on our mission."

"I will!" cried Johnny. "I swear I'll be with you that morning, and I'll follow you anywhere in the whole world."

"My blessing on you, Johnny Cregan," the priest pointed again to the murky sky. "O Lord, I call you to witness that this man has made the sacrifice. Let the curse depart from him!"

After that, his departure with the priest never left Johnny's mind. He thought of it every minute in the day, until it began to blot out Rosa's face and the body of Neil Fogarty with the blood gushing from his ears.

Chapter XXXIII

Anna was capable of great perseverance and tenacity of purpose. She knew that Johnny had not resigned his post, and she knew also that he had not said a word to the sheriffs about his refusal to undertake Mrs. Fogarty's execution. So the day after Johnny's meeting with the priest, she tackled him again on the subject.

"Johnny, there's that execution on Wednesday. You're not really going to be silly, are you?"

He stared at her with peculiarly blank eyes.

"An execution on Wednesday? I'm glad you told me. It's odd, now, I didn't remember."

"Then you're going to take it on after all?" said Anna in amazement.

"Why wouldn't I be? You talk like a fool. But it's odd, I didn't remember."

He stared at the fire for a few moments, a puzzled look on his face. Then he turned abruptly and began to play with Michael's bricks.

"Well, now, who'd have thought it?" marvelled Anna to herself. "It just shows what crazy, contrary creatures men are."

She and the child were in fits of laughter over Johnny that evening.

He behaved in the most comical way, putting plates on his head and pursuing Michael round the table on his hands and knees.

It was exciting to run and run, with daddy coming quickly after you, his lips rolled apart and his eyes glittering like a real wild beast. Once Johnny's teeth caught the plump fugitive leg rather sharply, and Michael flopped down to nurse the bleeding gash, trying very hard not to cry.

Daddy did not seem to realise that the game had stopped. He still came on, breathing hard, and Michael screamed with real fear because daddy's eyes were contorted in a dreadful way with only the whites showing.

"Stop that now, Johnny," said Anna; "can't you see you're frightening the child?"

Daddy paused then and sat up, but he did not say he was sorry for biting Michael's leg. He only stared round in a dazed, puzzled way, and would not play anymore.

Still, it had been an enjoyable evening.

"Wasn't daddy funny to-night?" said the child as she put him to bed. "I wish he was always like that."

"Yes, indeed, it's nice to see him so lively. He's getting well at last—poor man."

The day before the execution, Anna got up early and went quietly about the room so that Johnny would not be disturbed.

He was sleeping like a child with his hands folded under his chin and a peaceful look on his face. She bent over him.

"It's nice to see him sleeping so sound. It's almost a pity he has to go to the prison to-day to get ready for the execution."

At that moment, he woke up and lay gazing about him with a rather dazed expression.

"You ought to be up early," said Anna; "you have to be at Portobello Prison to-day."

"That's so." He made as if to spring out of bed, and was suddenly arrested in mid-action.

"I wonder who'll lie with you in this bed?" he said dreamily. "It's sleeping under the hedge on the road I'll be, or in the field with the cows."

She shook him by the shoulder.

"Wake up, Johnny. You're dreaming still."

"Yes, I'll get up. Soon I'll be out of this, thank God."

Then sudden activity returned to him and he leaped out on the floor.

"Let you be getting the breakfast, Anna, while I'm putting on my clothes."

She went into the other room, and a moment later she heard his voice, on a shrill, cracking note:

"And then I hanged my Annie."

"Hush, Johnny!" she called; "you know I don't like that song."

He was silent then, and soon afterwards he came in, fully dressed.

"Give me three rashers," he said, "I'm hungry."

"Thank goodness he's getting well again," she thought, putting the bacon on to his plate.

He took one mouthful and pushed it away from him.

"I thought you said you were hungry," cried Anna.

"Is that what I said? I am not, then. I'm not wishful to eat at all."

Nobody spoke for a few minutes. Michael was devouring his bacon and a few cold potatoes from yesterday's supper, and Anna was bending over the fire.

Suddenly a laugh, as sudden as a pistol shot, rang out.

Anna turned sharply and saw Johnny staring up at the ceiling, his face convulsed with high-pitched laughter.

He stopped as suddenly as he had begun.

"What amused you so?" asked Anna.

"I disremember. It was very funny a minute ago."

"Well, it's nearly time for you to start."

"Shall I get your ropes and straps, daddy?" cried Michael. "I know where they are." He came and leaned against his father's knee. "I wish you'd take me with you, dad. I'd like to see someone hanged."

"You're not to talk like that," reproved Anna sharply.

Johnny was staring at the window, frowning a little, as if trying to remember something.

"Now, Johnny," she said, hustling up, "all your things are ready for you. Wear your big coat, for it's pouring with rain. You should be back by to-morrow evening."

"Yes, I'll come back," he said. "The day after, you'll be watching for me at the door, and I away in the fields or taking my way along the road out of this town."

She looked round the bare, dim little room.

"Yes, Johnny," she said, "maybe we could manage a spell in the country. It would be nice to see the fields again. I'm sick of this place too. Maybe we could sell the shop and make a fresh start somewhere else."

Johnny was staring vacantly again, not listening to her at all.

"Take care of the money, won't you?" she said anxiously.

"Oh, you and your money! Maybe you'll have money enough when I'm gone."

* * * * * * *

Hanging Johnny's method of execution had just one peculiarity. He always drew the white cap over the prisoner's eyes before they left the cell.

Thus it was that Rosa Fogarty on the day of her death caught only a glimpse of his face, and was sure she must be dreaming. She was half-fainting with nervousness, so she did not distinguish his voice from the others round her. The prison surgeon had said, the day before, that she was in too weak a state of health to sustain the sight of her executioner.

The execution was rather a perfunctory affair. The chaplain mumbled the prayers for the dying without much care. He felt that the woman was impenitent and intercession with her God could do little good for her.

But everything was carried out quite smoothly and properly, though some remarked to each other on the vacancy of the executioner's face and the mechanical accuracy of his actions.

It was when it was all over, and they were preparing to leave the scaffold house, that something happened which no official of the prison was ever able to explain.

The hangman glanced down into the pit. Then the empty, passive look passed suddenly from him. His face seemed to wake slowly to horror and memory and something else that was terrible. He gave a frightful heart-shattering scream and fled out of the scaffold-house too fast for anyone to follow.

"What on earth has happened?" cried the Sheriff, pulling himself together. "After that man, quick, somebody."

One of the warders rushed out, but the hangman was nowhere to be seen.

"It's terrible queer," said another warder, shaking his head. "I don't like the looks of it at all. There were tears pouring down the face of him."

* * * * * * *

That afternoon Anna was sitting by the fire, but she was not sewing. She had a notebook on her knee and she was making some calculations with a pencil.

"Ten guineas won't last very long," she reflected. "But that was a good idea of Johnny's—to go out into the country for a bit. Perhaps—perhaps father wouldn't be set against him so much now. We might go to Ballyboulteen and see. I feel as if I'd like to see father again. There's a time comes when you do get lonesome without your own folks—father was right. And the air would be good for Johnny. He would get well again once I got him away from that maniac of a priest, and we could make a fresh start—quite a new, fresh start."

A knock sounded sharply and suddenly on the shop door, which was closed.

"That can't be Johnny," she said to herself. "Besides, he wouldn't knock."

She put down the notebook and descended the stairs, half expecting to see Father Gilligan when she opened the door.

Instead there were two men supporting a prostrate figure.

She looked and grew pale.

"Has there been an accident?" she gasped. "Good God, is he dead?"

"Drunk as hell," one of the men said briefly. "We were at Megarty's when in he rolls, full enough to kill himself. There's great wonder he was able to stand. But, sure, nothing would do him only to get down another pint and then down he falls on the floor the way you're seeing him now. We knew he was your husband, ma'am, so we're after bringing him home the way you wouldn't be worrying over him."

He spoke kindly, but there was a certain exultation underlying his words.

"This will be a lesson to Mrs. Croghan," they had said to each other on their journey through the streets. "Always telling us how to behave ourselves, she was. 'Look at my husband,' she'd be saying to my wife and to yours. 'Has he ever the drink taken, or does he be gambling or stravaguing about with no back to the coat of him, the like of your men?' she'd be saying. Well, it seems that he's not so much better than the rest of us, after all. Kitty will laugh when she hears this."

Anna bent forward to look again.

Johnny's eyes were closed, but his face was purple and he breathed with difficulty.

At the same moment, the heads of Mrs. Donovan and Mrs. Doyle appeared at their respective windows. They stared very hard, but something—perhaps a warped instinct of chivalry—kept them silent.

"Can you carry him upstairs?" said Anna, holding her head very high.

Grasping Johnny rather carelessly by his head and feet the men laboured up the narrow, dark staircase and laid him on the bed.

When they had gone, she undressed him, and drew the blanket over his shoulders. He lay very still, breathing through his pale, open mouth.

"Whatever did he do it for?" she wondered, leaning over him. "It's the second time, too. He never used to touch anything before."

A sudden idea came to her and she picked up his coat and examined it. There was no money in the pockets.

"What can have happened?" she thought. "I'll ask Johnny all about it when he comes round."

She sat beside him for the rest of the day, often putting bandages soaked with cold water on his forehead.

About nine o'clock in the evening, she heard his breathing change. He had come out of his stupor and was sleeping quite soundly and sweetly.

"That's queer," she murmured, amazed at the sudden transition. "However, it would be a pity to wake him now. In the morning he'll tell me everything."

She began to undress at her usual time, folding her clothes neatly on a chair. Then she crept into bed and took one of Johnny's hands in hers, because it was very cold.

At half-past three in the morning, Johnny awoke. The fumes of the whisky had gone out of him, and he lay staring into the darkness. Then a thought began to take shape in the blankness of his mind. This was the time he was to go to Father Gilligan. He pulled his hand out of Anna's and got softly out of bed. It was pitch dark, but he managed to throw on some clothes. This was the time he was to go to Father Gilligan. It was the one thing in his mind. When he was dressed he stepped over to Michael's bed and took something that lay on the pillow beside the child.

Then he groped for the key hanging on the bed-post, found it, and stole downstairs.

He did not glance once at Anna or Michael as he left the room.

This was the time he was to go to Father Gilligan. A faint sound woke Anna, a sound like a cry.

"Is that you, Michael?" she said sleepily.

"I can't find my dolly, mother. Where has my dolly gone to?"

"Be quiet, Michael! We'll find your doll in the morning. It's very naughty of you to wake me up at this time of night."

"But I want my dolly—"

"Oh!" Anna gave a cry.

"Mother, what's happened?"

"Johnny's not here, he's not in bed. Wherever has he gone?"

She raised herself on her elbow and listened.

The raindrops pattered softly on the window-pane.

"Johnny! Johnny!" she called.

Silence.

Anna tumbled out of bed, lit the candle and ran into the other room. It was quite empty but a draught blew up from the shop as if the door was open.

"Mother," called Michael, "the key's not on your bed-post."

Anna ran back and began to put on her clothes, shivering in the chilly air.

"What are you doing?" cried the child.

"I'm going after daddy."

A horrible fear had taken possession of her. She knew, though she could not have told you how, that Johnny was with Father Gilligan.

Somehow the thought terrified her.

"The madman isn't safe. He may have got Johnny to come to him, just to—"

She began to get so frightened that she forgot to pin up her hair. She seized her cloak and ran down the stairs.

"Mother, come back," wailed Michael, but she took no heed.

The shop door was open, swinging crazily on its hinges. A spurt of rain caught her in the face as she looked out.

"Oh, I'm behaving like a fool," she said, trying to calm herself. "Johnny has just gone for a walk because he couldn't sleep. He'll be back in an hour, maybe. I'd better go to my bed again, I don't know what frightened me so."

But, as she turned away, something lying in the gutter caught her eye, and she picked it up.

It was a silk handkerchief, all muddy and discoloured by the rain.

As she held it in her hands, all her terror rushed back. She closed the door and began to walk rapidly along the street.

"Johnny's with the priest. I know he is," she muttered to herself. Then some of Johnny's words on the day before Rosa's execution flashed back to her. "He said he was going away. Going away with the priest! Mercy of God, that's what he meant! I know now."

She did not stop to question the instinct that told her this. She began to run and run, clutching the handkerchief in both hands.

"Lord send I'm not too late," she prayed. "Don't let me get there after they're gone. Oh, if I can make Johnny come back with me!"

She knew the way to Father Gilligan's little hut on the quays. She ran and ran till she choked for want of breath.

Dawn was just creeping in, when she came in sight of it—a round, one-storeyed structure.

The door was open and she thought she saw a figure through the dim light.

"Johnny!" she called sharply.

The figure moved towards her, and she saw who it was.

"It is I," said the priest.

"Where's my husband? Did he come here?"

"He came—yes."

Father Gilligan stood in the narrow doorway so that she could not see past him into the house.

"Why are you here?" he said in his deep, mystic voice.

"I came to find Johnny, I knew he was with you."

The priest did not move.

"Let me see him at once," she said, a sharp note of fear in her voice.

He regarded her, with something almost like pity.

"You had better think before you wish that," he said.

"What do you mean? He isn't dead?" That was the most awful thing she could think of.

"It would be a better thing for him if he were dead."

"What do you mean? Let me go to my husband at once."

She stepped forward as if to push him out of her way, then something in his face made her hesitate.

"You were taking him away?" she said in a whisper.

"I was taking him with me out of this city. Together we would have carried the message. He came this morning as he had promised."

"And you haven't started?"

"He can never come with me now."

Then Anna's fears and anxiety took the upper hand. She sprang at the priest, beating him with her hands.

"Let me see him at once. Let me see him at once. You cruel, wicked creature, what have you done to Johnny?"

He held her away from him, gripping her hands with a strength amazing for his gaunt frailty.

"I have done nothing," he cried. "Listen, woman, it is the curse of God that has fallen on him for his work as a hangman. He took up his penance too late, and he has been punished."

He moved suddenly out of the doorway, and Anna wrested herself free and looked into the passage. What she saw made her start back with a cry.

Then, as she began to understand, she grew very slowly white.

"You see what has happened," said the priest. "It has been coming upon him for many days." If he had known about the murder of Neil and Rosa Fogarty, he would have danced and shouted in the grey dawn, for his theory was proved triumphantly in the face of the whole world.

But that would not have comforted the poor woman who stood watching Johnny solemnly hanging a rag doll from a nail in the wall by a piece of old charred rope.

THE END

www.ingramcontent.com/pod-product-compliance
Lightning Source LLC
LaVergne TN
LVHW031606060526
838201LV00063B/4747